Time Stop

Doug Harle

DEDICATED TO:

My Wife

My Daughters

My Grandchildren

"Time Does not Stop"

ACKNOWLEDGMENTS

Many Thanks to Vicky Peplow
For all of her help and
editing skills

Timestop

Chapter 1

The doors crashed open as the paramedics raced
through the corridor towards an A&E department
practically bursting at the seams, at Ashford General.
"Cardiac Arrest!" shouted one of the paramedics.
The crash team moved instantaneously into action,
like ants around their new arrival.
"Listen up" the authority of a senior doctor called
out.
"We've got John McAndrew, arrested twenty
minutes ago, re-sussed by medics, and has relapsed
again." A string of medical jargon followed; each
piece digested by the carefully placed professionals.
Machines buzzed and beeped into action, to save this
young man's life, which sadly, was slowly slipping

away from him.

Senior A&E Doctor, Dr James Wilde, was now calling the shots, machine gun like instructions were being followed to the letter by his colleagues. As the valuable seconds turned into long minutes, that were slowly ebbing away, there was no respite in the anxiety for their patient. As if time had given those around him a limited slot, the pinging of the heart monitor was no longer echoing round the room, it had suddenly changed to a straight deathly tone, just an alarm light flashing. They all looked around at each other, no response from the team, and no response from their patient. Despite all the efforts, it looked like Mr McAndrews, was to be another sad statistic of death by cardiac arrest.

Dr Wilde spoke those inevitable words, "Let's call it, no pulse, no brain activity. It's been too long now. Time of death, 12.45p.m." As he removed his gloves and gown, he looked around at his team and said, "Thank you for all your efforts, but let's move along quickly, the world doesn't stop here."

Assistants began removing the vital pieces of

equipment that had been John's only hope of survival. Just a short while earlier, he was Mr Average, having his lunch in the local park, watching the world go by until, like a lightning bolt, a sharp pain to the chest, his fight had truly begun. The doctor moved quickly on to the next cubicle, where one of the many other patients waited for attention and expertise. Following a quick diagnosis, he passed his findings for one of the nurses to follow up.

Suddenly, the arrest buzzers went again. He immediately turned and raced up the corridor, nurses and assistants appeared from nowhere, all heading for the resus area at the top of the hall. Dr Wilde was first at the room only to find a distressed assistant pressing the alarm button and blabbering on, with little or no sense about the deceased Mr McAndrew.

"What is it woman?" he said tersely.

In complete and utter disbelief, she stuttered, "He... spoke... to... me..."

"Impossible…" replied the doctor, "…this man is dead."

He realised how rude he had been and now felt guilty for speaking to the young lady this way. So, he put a reassuring arm around her and realized what had happened.

"What you may have heard, was probably the remaining air in his lungs leaving the body."

"No" she said adamantly.

He looked at the body of the patient, then back to the young lady with a soft smile,

he walked over to the body that he had not long-ago pronounced dead.

The doctor lifted the covering sheet from Mr McAndrew's body, and placed his fingers on the neck searching for a pulse. He wasn't sure, but there was indeed something faintly there. His years of medical experience sped through his brain, and he thought to himself, this cannot be happening, this is impossible, but his trained finger nerves were telling him something different. A string of medical commands followed, and once again the team surged into action, albeit a little confused.

The equipment tracers pulsed once more, and churned out their bits of paper information into the doctor's hands, giving him positive information. He couldn't believe what he was seeing, this could not be right. He shouted out orders to administer the vital lifesaving drugs once more.

He examined the patient's responses with scrutiny. Suddenly, the heart monitor burst into its traditional song... beep, beep, beep. Normal rhythms and beats were indicated on the screen. Dr Wilde stared at it, as if it dared to interrupt his thoughts. As more and more equipment was being attached to John, the more of a mystery it became. More drugs were administered, John's body began to convulse, writhing back and forth as if life itself was being forced back into it. After a while he eventually calmed, and the machines went into regularity beeping rhythm as if nothing had happened, as if time had reversed.

Dr Wilde left his staff to stabilise the patient and headed to his cluttered office. Bewildered, he sat and stared at the admission notes, probing his brain to find some logic on how this twenty-six-year-old, fit young man, found unconscious, with no signs of drug misuse, no alcohol present in his system but his deep thoughts were going to be stopped by a sharp knock at the door.

"Come in." as the door began to open, he noticed it was his friend, hospital consultant, Doctor Peter Grant.

"What the hell's going on Jimmy? I've just heard what happened and nobody else can believe it."

"I know." said James, he was trying to understand it himself. "We worked on him for over thirty minutes, he was clinically dead for ten minutes, and lay in the cubicle for at least twenty, it's physically impossible. Look at him now Peter, all his vital signs are spot on, it's as if he hasn't been here for treatment.

How the hell am I going to write this one up? I don't know where to even begin but I know one thing for certain ....in my entire medical career, I have never seen anything like this. I just can't explain it, but I do know that this department has just witnessed a real miracle, and for whatever reason, this man was destined not to die today."

Chapter 2

John stared out of the lounge window, watching the trees swaying back and forth in the early spring winds, their motion seemed very soothing to him, certainly better than any medication the hospital could supply. Scrap books and cuttings on the desk revealed, John had been a bit of a celebrity during the past twelve months, local headlines revealing the nature of the interest with lines like, "Hospital staff say, "It's a Miracle" or "Back from the Dead" etcetera.

Following months of exhaustive tests, none of the hospital doctors could explain the events of that day, their combined knowledge revealed he was as fit as any man of his age, and there was no reason to suggest in the future he will have any recurrence, or indeed, any related problems at all.
John also could not explain that day either, all he

could recall was, he in the park, and then the pain. There wasn't any "into the light" moments, angels, tunnels, or any directions to the pearly gates. The press had tried so hard for that exclusive "Near death experience story," but John could not satisfy their journalistic needs. I suppose it would have been easy to make one hell of a tale for them, but that wasn't John McAndrew. He couldn't lie about something he couldn't understand himself, or indeed why it happened at all.

His daydream broken by a distant voice. "Do you want a beer, coffee or tea?"
It took him a second to realize who it was. "What? Oh yeah… I'll have a beer thanks sweetheart."

As if on cue, Johns wife Lilly came into the room, complete with a large glass of beer.

"Hi darling, how have you been today? By the way, I picked up the new medication Dr Wilde has prescribed for you; he said this should help with your sleep."

John looked at her in an incredulous way. "They don't know, do they? I tell them what is happening to me and they take no bloody notice. They just fob you off with tablets, fill you with medication and say well that's him cured."

"They are trying their best John." His wife replied. "Lil, like I told you before, they don't give a shit, they have had their publicity out of this. it makes them look very proficient in front of the press, but it's been a year since my cardiac arrest, and they are no further forward with either an explanation or a diagnosis. My dreams are so vivid now, it's the same bloody dreams night after night and the headaches just get worse, how could they say, what's happening to me now, in their eyes is normal?"

A long and sustained silence took hold between them…John wrapped his arms around Lilly, "I'm very sorry sweetheart, I shouldn't take my frustrations out on you, …. I don't know where this is all coming from."

Lilly smiled reassuringly. "It's okay, John." Lilly considered her next sentence very carefully.

"John, do you think we should look for help somewhere else for the answers you need?"

"Like where Lilly and like who? Do you mean a shrink or something? I'm not bloody crazy if that's what you think."

"No, John. I didn't mean that. Just maybe, there could be someone out there who may understand your problems a bit better."

Lilly knew this entire experience was getting to John, depressing him to no end, and yet he was right, no one had come up with any answers for the problems he was having, or how it happened in the first place. All the medical knowledge at that huge hospital and yet, no answers, or answers they were prepared to share with them.

She was concerned too, that the whole thing was steadily getting worse and it had gone on long enough now, it was starting to affect John mentally. She hugged and kissed John, giving him a reassuring smile.

"Right, first thing tomorrow, I'll check it out with the hospital."

"Mrs McAndrew, you can go in now." smiled the receptionist.

Lilly tapped at the door of Dr James Wilde. "Come in Lilly, how are you today?"

"Doctor, I'll get straight to the point." she said in quite a stern manner. "I've been coming to this hospital for almost a year to discuss John's condition, and it seems to both John and I, we are not getting anywhere fast, nothing is improving at all. He still complains about his restless nights, vivid dreams and headaches, and to me, he is only being treated as any other cardiac arrest patient, which I am sure you are aware he is not. I know John better than anyone else and believe me, he is a fighter, but I think the after effects of his trauma are starting to affect his mind."

Doctor Wilde sat attentively listening to Lilly's list of John's symptoms, just stopping occasionally to scribble notes on a jotter pad.

"I'm so worried about my husband, Doctor, his whole behaviour has changed, and he gets so angry at times. When he talks to me, he sounds so bitter, it's just not like him, it's certainly not the man I married four years ago."

Lilly could feel herself becoming angrier the more she spoke. "Why has he changed so much, where has my husband gone? Dr Wilde, where.?"

Dr Wilde said nothing, for what seemed like an eternity, and then he opened Johns case note files. He scanned the pages, flicking them to and fro, as if they were going to tell him something new. He sat upright in his comfortable chair.

"Mrs McAndrew, this case has baffled not only me, but many doctors in this hospital, and many of our colleagues in the medical community globally. What I can tell you for certain is, all the medical facts add up to nothing...absolutely nothing. John is quite unique, I know, because I was there, on that night he "recovered" beyond normal medical boundaries. John was clinically dead Mrs McAndrew, for over thirty minutes and in these circumstances, no one would survive or recover, not at least without encountering some sort of brain damage. There have been historical cases where patients have all the symptoms of death. No pulse, no brain activity and consequently have been certified dead only to recover in the mortuary, this is known as "Lazarus Syndrome" but Mrs McAndrew, none of these had undergone actual cardiac arrest."

He reviewed the notes and reeled off the circumstances. "Your husband's heart had already stopped when the paramedics got to the park to assist him. He was shocked and defibulated four times and his heart was only kept in rhythm through artificial means. By the time he got to hospital, the chances of his survival were less than five percent. Perhaps you can see why, Mrs McAndrew, this case has mystified some of the best doctors in the world."

After scrolling through the notes, a little longer, he continued, "Following his recovery, he has undergone every test known to us. Scans, x-rays, blood, urine, toxicology, and ECG's. Every test we've done would suggest he is a healthy young man, nothing abnormal at all. The continuing dreams he is having, I can only assume, must be recalled from the deepest parts of his memory, brought on by the obvious trauma that came with his encounter. As a result, it would be foolish to think that tiredness, fatigue and restless nights, would not bring with it it's fair share of headaches to some degree."

Like a minister ending his sermon, he closed the file and paused. He stared at the tearful Lilly. "I can see the obvious concern you have for your husband, and I really wish I could help you more, but all I can suggest to you both, would be, to perhaps have some sessions with a psychologist or psychiatrist who may be able to help with this deep memory problem. If you want, I can arrange a consultation at the soonest possible date."

Lilly looked at the doctor disappointingly, tears dripping from her cheeks, she was hoping for something better from him. "An instant cure would have been nice!" She had cared for John all this time, and now she feared the worst, that this was the best it was going to get for John. She wondered how she could approach this subject with her husband, whose logic and patience had gone out of the window lately. How would he react to a "shrink" as he calls them? Her troubled face nodded in agreement with the doctor, and she said her goodbyes to Dr Wilde.

Chapter 3

Fields of red poppy's extended across the landscape like a magic carpet over the hills. A pink mist appeared from the top of the sky, getting lower and lower, it suddenly turned bright red, then a very deep blackness ensued, blotting the vision, which at first seemed, so breath-taking. John's heart began to pump faster, his pulse racing like a V8 engine. Perspiration cascaded from his brow and down his cheeks. The images in his mind came to an abrupt halt, and John's ordeal suddenly stopped. He sat up in bed, his face soaked with moisture, his mind still working overtime, although he was now wide awake. Lilly drowsily turned towards him, "Are you okay, sweetheart?

"What? Oh yeah, just the bloody dreams again. You go back to sleep, I'm okay.

Lilly rolled back over into her comfortable position and mumbled, "Okay."

John looked at the clock and the green neon light

displayed 2:10 a.m. A sight he was seeing more and more often these days. It was like the clock was becoming his best friend. Every night, they would meet at the same time.

He sat on the edge of the bed, his head beginning to throb like a bass drum. He raised himself from the bed and headed for the bathroom for his usual dose of medication. His eyes slowly adjusted to the strong light. John looked intently into the mirror inspecting a reflection of a man that was once so fit and rugged. God, he looked like shit these days, what the hell had happened to him? He retrieved his tablets from the cupboard, and was about to take the prescribed dose, when out of the blue a new symptom raged around his body, a feeling he had never encountered before. It cascaded through his body and he felt like he was weightless. Tiny bright lights began flashing on then off round his eyes, like twinkle lights on a Christmas tree.

"What the hell is going on?" he thought. *"Is this it? Am I going to die?"*

He was just about to call for Lilly, when all the activity abruptly stopped. So quickly, it was as if someone had pulled the plug out of the wall socket. He again checked himself in the mirror, pulling his cheeks down and his eyelids up. He was okay, in fact feeling quite well.

"What was this all about?" he wondered, *"Maybe the medication is starting to work, or maybe I've just been too impatient."*

John realised that his headache had dissipated and decided against taking the painkillers. He made his way back to bed and had a quick glimpse at Lilly to make sure he hadn't disturbed her once again, but she was fast asleep. He climbed back into bed to try and get a little extra sleep and he would tell Lilly everything later when they were both up about what had occurred. He glanced at his new trusty neon green best friend, it still read 2:10 a.m....

Lilly was up early, cooking breakfast, when John appeared in the kitchen, "God, I feel really crap this morning Lilly, but I've got so much to tell you about last night."

"I've also got something I need to talk to you about as well, John." Lilly turned the eggs over and said, "Okay, you first, was it your dreams again?"

John relayed the story exactly as it unfolded during the night, but confessed, I thought it was the start of something good Lilly, "I thought I'd feel much better today. Do you think the medication is starting to make a difference?"

She thought for a while. "Well it may be but I just don't know. You need to remain optimistic about anything good, no matter how small." John stared at the newspaper, as if he was reading it, but all the time in a morning trance and memories of the night.

"Well, what's your news sweetheart?" He asked his

wife

Lilly sat down, "Do you want some toast?"

"No thanks."

"How about some freshly made coffee?"

Again, "No thanks"

"What about some juice?"

"Lilly!"

Frustrated he said, "What the hell's the news? Are you going to tell me or is it 20 guesses?"

"Okay, okay. I went to see Dr Wilde yesterday, there is no easy way of putting this, but he thinks the only way forward is consultation with a psychologist or psychiatrist." A long silent pause followed.

"A shrink! will they be able to solve my problems, will they? Is that what he thinks?"

"John, calm down, he said all the tests they have done prove you are as fit as the next man, they can't find anything wrong with you."

Pondering his options, thinking profoundly, *"Do I dig my heels in and decline this wonderful offer and eventually go mad? or is Lilly right, are my options limited?"*

Johns brain was see-sawing between his choices, as always Lilly would be right. She wouldn't have given up easily with Dr Wilde. She would have asked all the possible questions and would demand the answers. Anyone would want Lilly in their corner, she could handle any issue, cool on the outside, but fierce on the inside. She wouldn't stand for any nonsense…from anyone. Anyway, he guessed she would have already made the appointment!

Following what seemed like an eternity, John smiled at Lilly. "Right then woman, a kiss and off to the nuthouse I go." She leapt across the table and hugged John.

Smothering him in loving kisses. "I take it, you have booked me in?"

"Of course." she replied, "We are going to try a well-known recommended psychiatrist, Dr Isaac Goldsmith. I'm sure it will be okay, and maybe it's the best way forward John."

"Right, okay, you know best. Oh, I forgot, on the way there, we need to get a new alarm clock. It gave up the ghost last night."

Lilly was washing up, "Well it must have fixed itself, because it's working okay this morning.

Chapter 4

The car turned into a tree lined winding road, continuing until it reached the entrance of a grand country house, which had probably been owned by some privileged family in the past. Now it was the clinic of Dr Isaac Goldsmith, a well-known member of the psychiatrist fraternity.

Lilly stuttered, "John, I'm a bit nervous about all this but don't worry, everything will be fine. Just remember, it's our chance to get to the bottom of all of this, and get you better." John looked intently at the big brass sign on the doorway. The only word that rang alarm bells in his head was "Psychiatrist".

His mouth was dry and beads of sweat hung on his forehead, "I feel awful Lilly."
"Stop worrying." she asserted.

After sitting for what seemed an eternity, a receptionist called their name, "Mr and Mrs

McAndrew, 4:20p.m. appointment. Just along the corridor and it's the room on the left."

John stared at Lilly in a closed teeth voice. "I need to go to the toilet."

"For god's sake John, you would think it was your first day at school." She continued, "Okay, but please be quick, these people are very busy."

He made his way to a plush looking "Gentlemen's Room." He looked in the mirror at his sweltering brow and just then, like a reminisce moment. The flashing lights in his eyes he recollected from last night, started all over again. *"Oh no! he thought. Not now, I'm going to be in a right mess by the time I see this damned doctor."* Moments later, the lights ceased, just like they did the previous night. *"Right,"* he thought having outstayed his welcome and how anxious Lilly would be, *"let's get this over with."* He walked out of the toilet, with the door banging behind him, only to observe an eerie silence.

He looked around, people were there, but not moving or saying anything. What had been a busy place, had turned into total standstill. He made his way across the hall looking left and right at the silent motionless people, across to the receptionist, who had been so helpful before, but she stood motionless, almost like a shop mannequin.

'Excuse me." But no reply. Her facial expression did not change one bit.

"Excuse me, could you tell me which room I have my appointment in?" but still nothing.

Puzzled he looked around; the people remained motionless. What the hell was going on? Walking down the corridor, he checked the first room he came to, empty. He moved to the opposite door, and there was Lilly. A small spectacled man was looking in his diary behind a very large desk, again totally still.

"Lilly!" John shouted but there was no reply.

John walked across the room and faced Lilly. She sat there just staring at the doctor, unmoving. John grabbed her shoulders and shook her but still nothing. "Lilly, for god sake say something. This is not funny anymore."

Filled with panic, he darted out of the room and returned to the toilets, immediately splashing water all over his face. *"I must be dreaming, or I've passed out or something."* Drying his face, he looked into the mirror, *"Am I going mad? Am I really going mad? Is this just the beginning?"* He continued looking in the mirror, *"Is a pair of big male nurses, going to come in here, grab me, and whisk me off to the padded cell any moment?"* He began pacing back and forth, *"What the hell will I do? This has to be a bad dream."*

He slumped to the floor, head in hands, and pondered what to do next. *"Lilly will think I've passed out, come in and get me."* he thought. He sat and waited, and waited a little longer, but Lilly didn't appear. After a while he calmed and tried to think rationally, *"No good sitting here feeling sorry for myself. I have to try again."* he thought.

Slowly he opened the toilet door to the outside world, and somehow, everything was back to normal with people chatting in the waiting area, receptionists answering the phones. What was all this about? what had just happened to me?

He remembered the room where Lilly was with the doctor and walked straight in, expecting some sort of reprimand from Lilly because of the length of time he had taken.

"Hello John, let me introduce myself. I am Dr Isaac Goldsmith." John felt drained and bewildered, when he eventually shook the doctor's hand. He thought to himself, *"I pray to god this man can help me because this can only be madness and I am in the epicentre. I need someone to get me out of all this."* His appointment commenced.

Chapter 5

Lilly sat at her desk and looked intently at the clock on the wall in her office. Her mind was in the fast lane of a million imperative things. A friendly familiar face came to greet her,

"Hello, hello, anyone in there? Come on Lil, let's get a move on. I'm starving. Can we go and get some lunch?" Her long-time closest friend Amy Spence, gave her a gentle nudge. "Are you okay?"
"What? Oh, yeah I'm okay." she replied gingerly.
"Let's go then."

Hemsley Park was their destination, just across the road from the office where they both worked. They strolled around the park for a while and then sat down near the lake.

"Well then?" Amy inquisitively.
"Well then what?" Lilly replied.

"You've been too quiet over the past few days. I know you too well and I know you're up to something. She asked with a smirk on her face. "What's the secret then? Are your pregnant?"

With a look of shock on her face, Lilly replied, "No, not at all. I should be so lucky."

"What is it then, I know you're not yourself, is it work? Amy asked.

"No. Stop asking questions Amy."

"Lilly, you know me better than that, any secrets you have, are safe with me. We have known each other for too many years for bloody secrets, you know I tell you everything, like the time..." her conversation stopped abruptly as Lilly burst in unstoppable tears, she was wailing uncontrollably.

"Hey, come on Lil. What the hell's wrong?" Lilly was trying to explain her outburst, but couldn't get it out, half words mingled with sobs, tears and huge gulps of air. "Calm down my darling, calm down." Amy wrapped her arms around Lilly to console her.

"Where's all this come from? Lilly tried to pull herself together, but she was finding it hard to explain the pent-up frustrations and emotions she had kept deep inside for months.

"I don't know where to start." she said.

"I think you'd better start from the beginning." replied Amy.

It had been four months since the first visit to Dr Goldsmith, her torment had been none stop since that day. "I think he is going mad Amy!"

"Don't tell anyone Amy, he tried to explain to me that he thinks he has a "gift" and he can stop time. Can you believe that? It all started at the clinic, the very first visit…" she told Amy about the episode at the clinic, her lips quivering with anxiety. "After that, the whole thing has just got steadily worse, the new medication he's prescribed makes him feel depressed, and he spends most of the day in the den. His moods change every day, and I just don't know what to expect when I get home. Sometimes he is talking normally and other times he is ranting about this new ability, he argues with me saying I don't believe him. We were talking last week about his job and how long he had been off work, he looked at me in a way I have never seen in him. he said, he had spoken to his boss on the phone, and he said, that he wasn't returning to work. How could he do that, never thinking of our finances he just did it. He said to me he wouldn't need work anymore with his newfound talent."

"What a load of bollocks. he's so disillusioned.

" I didn't know what to say and he had become so aggressive; I think he has Schizophrenia."

"So, what does the shrink say about it all? asked Amy.

"He thinks his initial assessment seemed to confirm John's illness was related to memory and the medication he prescribed would be the answer, although it does have some severe side effects. He's never mentioned his newfound skills to the doctor, and he prefers to go to the clinic himself now. But, unknown to him, I got in touch with Dr Goldsmith and told him about John's ranting, beliefs, and his attitude towards me, but he just fobbed me off, and put it down to the medication."

"Don't worry he'll pull through it. It may just take time."

"I put the phone down and thought, it was okay for him to say that, but he doesn't have to live with him. I don't know John anymore Amy. He has changed so much, in fact, last week, we were arguing as usual, and he attacked me. He grabbed at my throat saying horrible things, and saying I didn't believe him, because I think I am better than him. He is going nuts Amy. He's obsessed with this Timestop thing and he can't see how stupid it all is. I am really frightened of him now. You know, a few months ago, he could say sorry, but now he doesn't know what it means. I think there is only one road for us. Please don't tell anyone a word of what I've said today."

Tears burst forth again and Amy instantly wrapped her arms tightly around her, "Don't worry, we'll sort this out."

For a while, both the women sat motionless and said nothing, Lilly was relieved she had eventually got at least some of the worry and hurt, drained from her system. Amy was trying hard to understand how just a short time ago they were a match made in heaven, and even considered to be the perfect couple but yet it could be extinguished as quick as a candle flame, and how could John turn from a sensible logical loving man to this crazy disillusioned loony.

"Tell you what Lil, why don't you come over to my house tonight, I'll cook you a nice meal, and maybe we'll chat some more, have a couple of glasses of vino, you can stay over if you like." Lilly looked at her best friend's kind face and took a deep breath of utter relief she replied, "I would love to, but should we contact John?"

"Will John miss you?" Amy asked.

With her head hanging low, she replied, "I doubt it. He'll probably not even notice I'm missing."

Chapter 6

John sat alone in his den, surrounded by clutter, which normally would never be seen in his home; his tidiness and wellbeing now a thing of the past. His concentration was focused on his newfound ability. He was slowly becoming a recluse in his own quarters, with little time to deal with normality, John continued to have his "stoppers" as he called them, and they were becoming more frequent as the weeks went by. He felt so frustrated, not been able to control them and it was pushing him to the limit, both mentally and physically.

He thought, if it was at all possible to achieve anything out of this "gift" he needed desperately to learn how to control it, how to switch the "stopper" on and off like a light. He'd tried all sorts of experiments during his stopped time. Moving objects, opening doors, but when he returned to real time, everything was as it was before, nothing had changed. John knew, if this was the case, whatever this capability was, it would be no good to him, in fact, no good to anyone. He was convinced he could do something more with this, John pondered, why give someone a talent that was no good? he glanced at one of the many clocks and stopwatches surrounding him, like a constant reminder of time itself. "Oh shit, I'm going to be late for the appointment with the doctor."

John arrived at the clinic twenty minutes late, "Mr McAndrew for Dr Goldsmith." the receptionist studied her appointment schedule, like a cat stalking its prey. "Your twenty minutes late, we run a tight ship here, Mr McAndrew." she said in her receptionist type voice.

"I'm very sorry, it was the traffic." John was about to go into detail when she interrupted.

"You can go in next but you may be waiting a

while." The receptionist responded.

"Again, I am sorry," replied John, "to spoil your day." John was so wound up, he would have killed her if she had said anything more, he took a seat in the waiting room and waited.

He knocked at the door, and there sitting, as usual, the small spectacled man. "Sorry I'm a bit late for my appointment doctor."

"No need for apologies, please sit down. So, tell me, how have you been since…" he checked his notes, "two weeks ago?" John thought its shit or bust here and spewed forth his big secret that he had been harbouring for many weeks, into the lap of the doctor, in the hope that he may just understand it and perhaps believe him, unlike Lilly, who thought he was just crazy.

John launched into his stories, from the beginning, the bedroom, the first visit to the clinic and the experiments at home. Doctor Goldsmith listened intently, with just the occasional, "oh yes" and "right then". John eventually came to the end of his carefully rehearsed speech. "Well then doctor, what do you think?"

Dr Goldsmith cleared his throat, "How are you doing with your medication John?"

"Okay doctor, no problems," he said agitatedly, "What about my gift? my ability?"

The doctor looked straight through John, "Do you know what delusion is John?"

He waited a while before answering this loaded question, "Yes, I know what that is, are you telling me, all of this is a figment of my imagination, and all of this is really not happening at all?"
"Unfortunately. I'm afraid I am John. What I think is happening is, the medication is stimulating your perceptibility of what is true and definite or what is false and improbable. I think we may need to look at

an alternative treatment. I know one thing John, you're a realistic man, you know deep inside, no one could possibly do the things you are talking about. Think of it logically John, it's impossible."

John's blood pressure was rising rapidly, his anger and frustration was growing inside him. With a raised voice John said, "How could that be and what if I can prove this is not in my imagination!"

The doctor was starting to feel anxious, "It's no good getting angry at me, John. That will do no good, but, if you would like to try and prove it to me, go ahead and stop time if you can!"

John tried to relax but couldn't, his heart was pumping blood around his body at a phenomenal rate, He rolled his eyes back in his head and very soon the sparkles began to appear. A few seconds went past and John returned his gaze on the doctor, who was motionless, still and silent. *"What the hell am I going to do if this doesn't work, If I fail; this bastard's next move would mean a medical section for me."*

John leaned over the desk and picked up the case notes, carried them over to the other side of the office and left them on a chair. He returned to his seat and tried to relax again, he was anxious, and he knew this probably wouldn't work. He sat back in his chair, rolled his eyes back, the sparkles started once again and looked at the doctor, hoping for the best.

John couldn't believe his eyes, *"Oh my god, Jesus fucking Christ!"* the files were gone! He immediately looked around there they were, placed exactly where he left them. *"Jesus"* he thought to himself, I've done it.

He turned to the doctor, "Well then what do you think? where's my case notes doctor?" The doctor peered to the desk. "They are gone." John excitedly jumped to his feet, "There, the notes are there." He pointed excitedly to the chair, "I stopped time and moved them. They were in front of you, weren't they?" the doctor agreed. "Well then, my Timestop worked, I told you I wasn't making it up. Now you have to believe me."

Hoping for a positive answer, John waited in anticipation. After what seemed a lifetime, the doctor eventually spoke, "Nice trick John, but is that the best you can do?"

John retorted angrily, "Fucking trick. it's no trick Doctor Goldsmith. That was done by stopping time, I moved the files and then restarted time."

The doctor immediately changed the subject, "We need to look at your medication John." He started talking about what was available and different amounts, this talk slowly relapsed into a low hum in Johns ears. He wasn't listening anymore, more content with the fact that he knew he had done it, *"fuck the doctor."* His hearing resumed...."is that ok John?"

"Yeah, yeah, fine doc." smiling as he reached out for

a prescription the doctor was handing him. "See you in two weeks John, just take the medication and try your best to be realistic, think positive John and above all relax."

"Oh, believe me. I'll be thinking a lot more positive now doctor." John quickly walked from the office, clicking his heels on the way out of the clinic.

John opened the front door and headed straight for the den. He sat in his chair and pondered how it had worked and more importantly, why did it work this time. Looking out into the garden, his mind clicked into gear, and as if a final part of a jigsaw had been put in his hand, he remembered how he felt at the clinic. He remembered that his blood pressure had seemed sky high and must have something to do with it all so that must be the key and if his blood pressure is up, he must be able to move things and then, they don't return. That's it, it must be. Relieved, he started to get all the past few months into some sort of perspective. How it worked, would it be detrimental to his health? and by doing this, would it injure him at all? But his logic told him, this talent had two sides to it, and could be very dangerous if not considered properly. He thought, "*If my doctor doesn't believe me, and my wife thinks I am crazy, who could I possibly tell, without the consequences of a permanent home in the mental asylum.*" He decided he must tell no one. "*I must keep this a secret for the rest of my life.*" His mind was flowing with ideas and how he could make this gift work for him...

A small spectacled man mumbled to himself as he drove through the heavy traffic in town, reassuring himself that he would not be late for his appointment. Dr Goldsmith was not the greatest of drivers and judging by the number of car horns sounding and finger digits gestured, his fellow travellers had no respect for his skills either. As if by miracle he eventually reached his destination. A place he knew only too well, "The Old Mare" public house, a very dark place for him. He was scheduled to meet, what you could call his business partner, but this was no ordinary relationship. Dr Goldsmith's partner was a journalist called Jimmy Conran, who he had known for many years, in fact since the bad days, as he called them when, Dr Goldsmith was struck off the medical register in Ireland.

Jimmy had "assisted" the doctor into a new life in this country by falsifying records to get him into a reputable job at the clinic. This kindness was not intended to be a favour of any sort. Jimmy was too scrupulous for that, it was a noose, a noose that had remained around the Doctors neck ever since, like a chained servant or slave. The doctor knew this of course, but part of his demise in the first place was his greed and over-prescribing patients with restricted drugs for just that little bit extra cash but the only problem was, it turned sour on him when one of his rich clients who he had being treating, died suddenly. The inquest found the doctor to be at fault, which subsequently led to the doctor's removal from the medical register and a spell in an Irish prison. Falling on hard times, with large bills to pay the doctor was happy for Jimmy's help at the beginning and a little bit of extra cash for a few celebrity clients secrets, what was the harm, they would have been in the papers eventually anyway.

The Doctor made his way into the bar, a grim place, Nicotine stained walls washed into the 1930's wallpaper to great effect. A place with thousands of stories to tell with drink, drugs and gangsters of years ago. Scanning around the empty room, the smell of stale beer reached his nose; he immediately took his handkerchief to his face, like an aid worker in a leper colony.

Quickly he marched around the corner to find his associate seated at the corner table. The landlord Tony grunted at Goldsmith, "What's it to be?"

Nervously he replied, "Just an orange for me and…"

he nodded towards his friend "… and whatever…" he didn't get to finish his sentence.

"Come on you old scrote, sit down, I haven't got all day." Goldsmith complied with the order. "Well! Come on then, what have you got for me?" Jimmy Conran had been a small-time press hound for years, mainly court stories, petty theft but nothing meaty or remotely journalistic. He had no ambition whatsoever, making fast bucks was his way forward in life. He once said he wouldn't touch a good Fleet Street job as the stories were to clean and as he put it, "You'll never make money out of clean people."

Goldsmith cleared his throat, "I want good money for this one Jimmy, I mean it. That last one I gave you, and you gave me two hundred quid. Christ you really stitched me up there. I saw a flash in the nationals about it a day later, you must have made a few bob out of that one."

Jokingly in a mock Jewish voice Jimmy replied, "Hey, ma boy. We've all got profit margins". A few sips of beer were followed by a silence; Jimmy stared at the doctor. "God only knows why you have to sell yourself Isaac. I would have thought the money your make now, at that posh clinic would be very good. In fact, you should be making a bloody fortune, and shouldn't need to sell "other people's stories", so much for bloody doctors and confidentiality."

Dr Goldsmith interrupted, "You know I need the money. I'm bloody broke, and you know it's my gambling, so don't start all that with me you bastard. Your no goody two shoes. You would bad mouth your Mother for a tenner, and anyway, one day, I will be rid of you so fuck you, you Jewish bastard and let's get down to business before I belt you one."

Doctor Goldsmith told him of the last visit of John McAndrew, and the seemingly impossible things he had performed. He admitted the act that he put on for

John would have won him an Oscar, but admitted he was total amazed at the feat. He didn't think it was a trick but found it hard to understand how it worked. Jimmy looked at the Doctor in amazement, staring at the spectacled man, "Do you think I am a fucking idiot Isaac? Why would you think I'd even consider this story, after all the nutcase stories you have given me in the past? Who the fuck would believe it Isaac?"

"I just thought it may intrigue your readers." the doctor replied sheepishly.

Jimmy peered out of the heavily stained bar windows and then looked intently into the doctor's eyes. "He's not an amateur magician or something is he? Do you even believe him Doc and don't fuckin lie?"

"I think I do believe him." Isaac replied. A long pause ensued while Jimmy scratched his chin and rubbed his neck.

"I'll tell you what Isaac. I must admit one thing, you've never sold me a bum steer, so I tell you what, just because it's you. I'll take a gamble. Here's the deal, I'll give you twenty pound now and if it makes the nationals, I'll advance it to two hundred, how about that?"

The Doctor was about to utter a refusal but then remembered his latest outstanding debt letter which just arrived this morning, "I was expecting more Jimmy."

"I know you were Isaac, but that's my best offer, not unless you want to take it yourself to the nationals, which you are perfectly entitled to do but, they do ask questions Isaac. Questions, I am sure you would rather not answer."

The Doctor looked nervously around the bar with beads of sweat beginning to show on his brow, "Okay, the bloody stories yours, here's the details."

begrudgingly he passed a piece of paper across the table.

"Pleasure doing business with you, once again Isaac." They both finished their drinks and left together, albeit with vastly different objectives.

━━━━━━━━━━━━━━━━━━━━━━━━━━━━━━━━━━

John sat in front of the TV watching and digesting the six o'clock news. He was wondering to himself, where Lilly was. A thought that had gone from his mind lately, she was late yesterday from work and the day before she had stayed out, in fact she was always staying out these days. He wondered what was going on, he was blissfully unaware that Lilly was just getting on with her life, and in fact, she hadn't been home for weeks. Lilly had already reached the point where she could no longer communicate with John, as he'd been too aggressive when she had tried. He was so cold and selfish sometimes, and she'd found comfort in her friends and work colleagues especially Amy, who had been a godsend to her.

Her secrets had been safe, so far, and her circle of friends were unaware, and just thought John and Lilly were just going through a very difficult time. John was oblivious that Lilly had been staying with Amy for several weeks, his lack of interest in her had just rejuvenated itself now following his breakthrough, with the Timestop. Prior to that, he wasn't even interested where Lilly was or who she was with.

Yesterday's argument was still fresh in his mind, and logic didn't tell him why Lilly didn't want to know anything more about the time stopping idea. To him it was a breakthrough; to her it was the end of their marriage.

His head turned quickly around at the noise of the front door closing. "Lilly is that you?" silence…

"Lilly can we talk?" Lilly walked into the room, standing confident and strong she stared right through John. She couldn't be bothered with it.

"What?" she replied sharply.

"Could we talk please?"

"Why John, what's changed?"

"What's got you all troubled?"

"Our marriage is fucked up John, and you know what? I don't want to fucking fix it." Lilly was firing on all cylinders now; she was sick of all the hassle.

"Where have you been over the past few months? He asked.

"Wake up and smell the coffee John, it's over. You're an aggressive bully with stupid thoughts and ideas, that's certainly no good for me. Well, I've had enough John. I'm not playing your stupid fuckin games anymore. There's nothing wrong with you and your own Doctor has told you that." She was on a roll and didn't dare to stop, so she continued. "I've given you plenty of chances and you didn't give a toss. Well John boy, Mr Timestopper. You're on your own now. I'll be looking for somewhere next week, and then I will be out of your miserable little life for good." With the final comment, she headed for the spare room.

John turned to the TV screen once again. Lilly's words had no effect at all on John, his reality of his marriage and how his wife was feeling meant very little to John. He had fixed his obsession and that was the main thing, she would see soon enough.

Chapter 7

It had been several weeks since Lilly moved out of the house, she now lived in a pleasant flat, close to work and Amy's house. He hadn't heard anything at all from Lilly, but he did try on many occasions to contact her, only to be blanked by her, or told to "Fuck off." It was certainly over for the two of them or for the time being, he thought, in his naive way.

More important issues were unfolding in John's life. He had just received a final Mortgage demand on his house, and the bills were clocking up fast. Since quitting his job, the poor old bank balance had been declining quicker than a downhill skier, he needed to do something and fast. He pondered for a while on how he could make some money maybe using his talent maybe as a nightclub act or street entertainer, but something told him these ideas wouldn't work and he'd not raise enough cash for that. He had to use his talent for a bigger project.

In his thoughts, Johns values and morals were being tested to the limit. He'd never stolen anything in his life, but who would ever know? He began to format his daring plan, maybe just a small robbery; it would prove a theory that it worked and would earn him a few quid.

He poured himself a beer and switched on the TV, the local news was following a story about the redevelopment of the high street and how some of the bigger stores are willing to come to town. The camera panned up and down the street showing the relevant sites. One being a supermarket, privately owned, and the manager was groaning on about loss of trade. While the interviewer was talking his piece to camera. John's mind went into overdrive as thoughts began to form, *"Hmm, I wonder if that could be just the job for me."* John realised he was no villain and he didn't have a clue how to plan a robbery of any sort, but his mind convinced him otherwise, maybe he had just been watching too many gangster movies or Crimewatch programmes to comprehend what he was about to conceive.

The following day John made his way to the high street and stood opposite "Joes Supermarket" surveying the situation. He noticed that the shop had CCTV cameras on the outside covering the doors and had to ponder on this for a while. He knew he would have to stop time before crossing the road, do the job and then start time again. He made notes as he moved up and down the street, being careful not to look too suspicious. After several walks past the shop he entered and noticed there were 5 tills in operation, all very busy, and the store was well covered with security cameras. As he turned the corner, near the sweet counter he noted a security officer, working very hard, helping people pack their bags. He started mentally scanning all the areas of the shop which could be a problem. His adrenalin was now in full flow as he purchased a newspaper, sweets, and then casually walked out. He was turned on just thinking of what he was planning, and what he was about to commit. He knew if this didn't work, he would have no more problems as it would be straight to jail for him, but his confidence was so high, he knew he could do it; he knew he could pull this off.

John made his way home, plans in his hand and in his head and he thought the best time to do it would be Saturday, just before closing. "Shit! that's tomorrow." He said out loud to himself.

The alarm went off, it was 8:00a.m. said his trustworthy clock. John gazed at the ceiling. "If I don't get caught, then today's the day that I will prove once and for all, what my abilities are, and what I am capable of. It's the perfect crime. It's just a shame that when I've done it, I can't stand on the rooftops and say, "Hey, all you doubters I did that, just look in my bag to prove it."

John checked his watch, it read 5:20p.m. and he

knew the shop closed at 6:00p.m. Standing on the opposite side of the road, he looked around, it was a busy high street today, the shop looked crammed. People getting their weekly shopping, ready for the weekend, and hopefully spending lots of cash. John administered the medication that he bought from the internet to increase his flow of blood, raising the pressure; he knew it was now or never. He sat for a couple of minutes while his blood raced around his veins like a formula one car.

He started his procedure to Timestop. slowly everything went quiet, the cars stood stationary, the birds stopped singing, and shoppers remained glued in position. John grabbed his bag and entered the store, the same picture he found inside. He approached the first checkout and feeling excited, pushed the button to open the till draw. It burst open to revel wads of legal tender. He grabbed the notes and quite calmly moved on to the next checkout, removing all the notes as he had done previously. In his mind and his planning, he thought he should have been a bit anxious and even scared at this moment, but to his surprise, he wasn't. He looked back when he got to the final checkout, his sports bag busting with money, all denominations of notes. He coolly walked out of the shop and back to the position he was prior to stopping time. He relaxed and slowly came out of the Timestop mode and waited for alarms or something to go off but he heard nothing.

John sat motionless for about ten minutes, he could see in the shop there seemed to be a bit of a panic, with the manager and checkout operators waving their hands about. The customers were arguing, and total bedlam had set in. John realised his plan had worked perfectly, releasing a large lungful of air, he once again picked up his bag and casually walked down the road, hearing sirens in the distance. He thought to himself, *"I would love to be a fly on the wall in there when the police arrive. Good luck trying to work this one out."*

It had been seven days since the robbery, and John,

who was so sure of himself now, couldn't believe why his piece of work was not getting the attention he thought it would have. It had been on TV and in the local press, saying thirty-five thousand pounds had been mysteriously stolen from the supermarket, which he knew was a lie, as his holdall only contained twenty thousand. He knew this would have been down to the owner trying to defraud the insurance or something, but it didn't concern him. John thought it may have hit the national press and TV, but only a small piece was in the Daily Mail. The police meanwhile continued to make local enquires, but John knew he was in the clear, or surely by now, he would have had a knock on the door by now. He recognized that the Police would have nothing to go on at all, apart from CCTV which he knew wouldn't implicate him.

John's disposition was starting to change now, no longer did he think this was wrong, it was the contrary, he had enjoyed it, he enjoyed the thrill, he was the top man and he wanted to do it again. He was aiming to plan more and more raids, bigger hauls next time and maybe out of the area to try and throw the Police off any suspicions of a local being responsible. The first raid helped him recover from his money drought, but he thought, why not do some more, he would never be caught, or so he thought. John's mind was playing tricks with his beliefs and principles because if someone had believed in him in the first place, this wouldn't have happened. He thought, *"Why should I stop now? Anyone else in my position would do the same if they could?"* he was convincing himself that this was definitely the right way to do things.

The following month saw John commit another six robberies, all with various amounts of money, all different types of premises, shops, banks, jewellers, The Police were no further forward with their investigations and were baffled on how these offences were happening. John started to make the headlines with his crimes. The bank job he did was fifty miles from where he lived, and netted over seventy-five thousand pounds. John had completed a deposit slip at a desk and simply waited until one of the staff had to open the door to the rear of the counter to move through the bank, he stopped time and walked in. He stole all the notes from the first two clerks, turned and walked out, back to his original position then started time again. Being cocky, he even paid one hundred pound back into his account before suspicions were raised about the robbery.

That little jaunt made the TV programme, Crimescene Today, and all the national papers. The TV people reported that an experienced gang were responsible. These crimes were considered major incidents and the persons concerned should be apprehended as soon as possible. John was thrilled at the statement and who are these people looking for really? He looked in the mirror; *"It's me"* he said to himself in a mad sort of glee? His mind secretly wanted to phone the police to taunt them about it, but on second thoughts, he decided that would be very unwise, he didn't want to tempt fate.

Part of John was getting bored and tired. Although the crimes were successful, it didn't prove his true worth, and talent, after all, it's not as if he could tell anyone about it. He was at a bit of a loose end, what else could he do with this now that the novelty had gone?

Suddenly the phone rang, "Hi John." it was Lilly. John hadn't heard from her for over six months, "I'll get straight to the point John, as I would rather not talk to you. I've got something I need to tell you; I've met someone else and I want a divorce." There was a long silence, "John, did you hear what I've just said?"

"So, who's this Romeo, you've acquired then." He asked, "You didn't waste much time, did you? We've only been separated seven months." he said sarcastically.

"He is a guy who actually cares about me John, not

like you. You only care for yourself and I need to move on, and move on with someone who can show how much he loves me."

"Lilly, for better or for worse, that's what we promised each other."

"I know we did John, but it's gone and surely you can see that. We've nothing left to promise each other." An awkward silence came over as John didn't say anything so Lilly continued, "Look, I am going ahead with this whether you like it or not. Goodbye John." Lilly hung up.

John was stunned and raging mad, he smashed his glass of beer into the wall, in his disillusioned mind, the past few months had just been a hiccup in their marriage, not a major problem. John didn't realise how much he had let his marriage drift. Equally, his mind would not remind him of the times when he was physically aggressive towards her, and how terrified she had become of him.

These factors didn't enter the equation as far as he

was concerned, she should have been more loyal, maybe given it more time, and anyway, she should have listened to me, and believed in me, and we would have been alright. Johns emotions were dancing in the wind, up and down like swings in a park. One minute, he would be trying to make sense of it, the next he would be hostile and saying things like, "I'll show her what I can do, the fucking bitch." His ramblings and his drinking went on for hours. John's new skills had a dark side, his behaviour was changing, ticking like a time bomb in his head. His mood forever swaying back and forth, as well as adopting a couldn't care less, aggressive attitude. These were very dangerous times.

Dr Goldsmith opened the file of John McAndrew, scrolling back and forth through the case notes, a patient he hadn't seen for quite some time. He was checking the medication lists, for which no repeats had been collected. Rubbing his sweating brow, he wondered how John was doing without his daily fixes.

He looked out of the window to the dark night sky, musing over the memory when John proved his time stopping ability in the clinic. Scattered on the desk were the many news reports of the robberies that had taken place recently. On reading the stories he figured out there was only one person, one magician, who could possibly do this. The Doctor knew what he had seen that day. He wondered, if John could really do this and could he actually be linked to the robberies. Maybe John, was unique, maybe these powers did exist, but we just don't know how to harness them for some reason. The infamous extra human sense, could John possibly have this gift? and if it was him, who committed these crimes, what a perfect way to prove and make it believable to himself and others.

As usual the Doctor was thinking of only himself, maybe he could benefit, and clear his outstanding debts. He thought, there was a strong likelihood that John has not shown this ability to anyone else, and if so, he would be the only one who has seen it demonstrated. A scheming glow projected from the Jewish man's face. He checked the newspapers once more and saw each of the larger business that had been robbed, were offering quite substantial rewards for information leading to prosecution. Plotting as the good doctor usually did, he realised he must have evidence of the feat but to accomplish that, he would have to have the full cooperation of John. He pondered on John's mental state, would he be willing? Examining the notes, he thought of the one thing John wanted from the onset, someone to believe in him.

The doorbell rang at Johns home, as was the norm these days, Johns house was untidy, and it was easy to see, he was alone in this abode. John, beer in hand opened the door.

"Hello Doctor, come on in, what can I do for you?"
A different John, quite responsive and generally happy, something the doctor hadn't seen in him for a

long time.

Goldsmith seemed worried about this sudden change in attitude. "Hi John, I thought I better pop in as I haven't seen you at the clinic for several weeks now and was wondering how you are coping."

"I'm fine doctor, I feel much better now." John replied.

The conversation went on, mainly about John's anxious state and how the doctor was pleased with the improvements.

"John, I've got to ask you this. Remember when you came to see me and performed that trick, moving the files. Can you still do that?"

The doctor was unaware that John was already two steps ahead of him, and realised weeks ago, the only person in the world who had seen the Timestop process work was the doctor.

"Ah no. That was just a trick doctor, even you said that at the time."

The Doctor was uneasy that his plan wasn't even beginning to form. "But, can you still do it?" he asked in a jokey pushy way. John explained to him that the trick was shown to him by an old work colleague and that's what it was, an illusion, a trick. There was a silent moment and then the doctor replied, "I know you can do it John, and I know you have done something haven't you?"

John was beginning to get annoyed with the doctor and quite taken a back that he knew so much. His aggressiveness pushed to the front. "Look doctor, I don't know why you have come here, or what you are trying to insinuate, but I am telling you, it was a trick and only that."

The doctor took a gamble, "You did it didn't you? The robberies? It's okay. I believe in you now John, you've proved it, you have proven your ability."

He looked closely at the small spectacled man, "Listen for the last time and listen good, I've done nothing, nothing, at all and I would be really happy if you would LEAVE RIGHT NOW!" He jumped up out of his seat and grabbed the doctor by the coat, walking him towards the door. The doctor turned, "Okay, John, I'll go. I just wanted to let you know, that I do believe in you and I know you have a gift. I know what you can do." John opened the front door and said goodbye to Dr Isaac Goldsmith, "Yeah, sure." as he closed the door.

For the first time, he started realising his worst nightmare. The one person he tried to convince has now become the one person who could convict him. He was aware the doctor had problems, through gossip he had heard and that he was by no means "clean". His past thoughts of what to do with his talent, began to unfurl a sinister plot.To balance the books Dr Goldsmith would have to be taken out of the equation.

Chapter 8

John sat in his local pub, in his usual corner spot, complete with lunch, a pint of larger, and a newspaper laying in front of him. He began to read the updates of the recent spate of robberies. His mind was wondering what Dr Goldsmiths next move would be. He knew he was quite a determined man, and his recent visit to the house certainly wouldn't be the last.

Dr Goldsmith's determination had John worried and feared if he didn't talk it out with the doctor, which he was not going to do, Goldsmith would eventually go to the police. John knew he couldn't allow this to happen, and he had to do something about the doctor, before it got to that point.

His concerns quickly turned to himself, his health had been suffering since the constant intake of blood pressure tablets. He was aware that his body didn't need this kind of abuse. The time stopping process was also taking it out of him, the experiments he did, months ago, stopping and starting the time he found when the process was over, left him feeling drained and unwell. Although, he still couldn't understand the many questions he had been asking since the beginning, about why him or how does this thing work, he knew the process had its limits.

During the robberies his heart rate had practically doubled, which he assumed was the increase in his blood pressure. John wasn't in any way, shape, or form, a medical man and it was one of those medical problems he couldn't go to his medical centre for, so he relied on information from the internet and books on the subject. He had discovered the longer he held time off, it was making him feel more unwell. He hadn't dared risked taking the Timestop to its limits, as this was an area that he knew nothing about. The only thing he was sure of at the present time was he could cope with about ten minutes maximum and then time must be restarted or who knows what could happen to him.

His sinister side of his mind turned towards the Goldsmith again. *"How am I going to get rid of this bloke?"* An opportunity must arise that will firstly, not put me in the frame or anywhere near it. he thought he could make it look like an accident or even suicide, he needed time, which he knew he didn't have much of. he needed to think quickly and get it done. John's mind suddenly switched into normal mode. *"God, I can't believe this, one minute I am an ordinary sort of bloke, with an ordinary life, now I commit robberies and plan murders, what has this time stopping thing done to me."* He got up and headed for the door. His mind was awash with all the things he had done, just for the sake of a talent which he couldn't understand or tell anyone about, it was crazy.

The phone had been ringing for what seemed like ages, and then at the other end, "Hello, Dr Isaac

Goldsmith, how can I help you."

"Hi, Doctor, it's John McAndrew. I was wondering, following our conversation the other night and I apologise for being so uptight, I was hoping I could come around to talk."

"Yeah, that's no problem John. Let me look in my clinic diary and see where I can fit you in."

John suddenly stopped the doctor mid-sentence. "No, no what I meant was, can I come around to your house, maybe tonight?" John waited for what seemed like a lifetime. Finally, the Doctor replied uneasily, and said that would be okay.

"Do you know where I live John?"

"Yeah, your house is opposite my local pub and I've got to go there tonight anyway."

"Okay, I look forward to it. I'll see you about seven. Oh, by the way, I'll be round the back so just come through the side gate."

"Okay, I will. See you then."

John took the mobile phone he had been using into his garage, placed it on the bench, and smashed it all to bits. After carefully putting all the broken pieces into a plastic bag, he went back into the house to get ready for his little jaunt.

John wandered up the street towards his local pub; already questioning himself if this was the right thing to do but he knew he had no other option. Looking at his watch it was 6.20 p.m. as he walked up to the bar, "Hi Tony, pint of larger please. Do you know if Tom is coming in later? I've got some information on that laptop he was after?"

"Yeah, he was in this afternoon and he hoped you would be in." Tony replied.

"Cheers mate." John responded, thinking to himself and the first part of his alibi.

The good doctors house was about five minutes' walk from the pub, so John took his usual seat and tried to calm his nerves, all the time thinking what he was about to do. John started drinking his beverage, but it didn't taste good but then, the whole evening didn't taste good, he just wanted it to be over. He once again checked his watch, six minutes to seven, he finished his drink and went to the bar.

"Another larger please Tony." the barman started to pour his drink.

John went into Timestop and the place fell deathly quiet. He walked out of the bar and quickly made his way to the doctor's house. He was starting to feel out of sorts, his blood pressure racing, trying the best he could to get to the Doctors as quick as he could. Everything was still as he entered the Doctor's property, up the drive; he noticed the side gate open. He walked up the side of the house into a beautiful garden area, where, he saw the Doctor, motionless standing near to his conservatory.

Wasting no time John rushed up to the Doctor and gave a glance around the premises, he placed his hand in his jacket pocket, and revealed a large kitchen knife. He swiftly stuck the knife into the Doctors throat with surprise, and relief, there was no blood had something went wrong? He thrust the knife once more into the side of the Doctors neck and then across it. Again, no blood. *"What the hell!"* he thought. He checked his watch; it was getting near eight minutes since he had stopped time. He brought the knife across the Doctors throat leaving a large gaping wound, but still no blood. Not wasting any more time to think about if it had worked or not, he put the knife into his inside pocket, then left.

He ran from the garden and back into the street, everything remained silent as he started making his way back to the pub. When he got to the pub door, he wasn't feeling well at all, but he knew he had to finish this, or it would have all been for nothing. He quickly dried the sweat from his face and made his way back to the bar where Tony was as still as the glass he was holding. He gathered himself and went into the process to start time.

"Do you want tonight's paper?" asked Tony. Time had restarted.

Stuttering slightly John replied, "Yeah, cheers mate."

The barman passed the newspaper and John returned to his seat, his heart beating faster and faster, he thought he was going to die. He couldn't get the image of the Doctor out of his head, but he knew he would have to remain balanced, at least for the next hour or two.

"Hi, John." A familiar voice spoke. It was his mate, Tom, "have you got that info mate?" They stayed and chatted for a while about everyday things, John not believing how he could be so cool after what he had done, or even if it had worked at all. Tom's voice went into the distance while John's mind went around all the details about tonight, he was covered, not with blood but a cast iron alibi, which, even if the police suspected him, they would never be able to prove.

A small spectacled Jewish man lay in his garden surrounded by a thick lake of blood which stretched out across his patio like a small red island. His body appeared as if it had been ravaged by a pack of wolves, his head practically decapitated from the rest of his body and his worries of debt no longer mattered to him. He was now at peace, unlike John McAndrew, whose sick mind hadn't allowed him to feel the consequences of his brutal actions. More concerned about covering his tracks, the actions of tonight would haunt him forever.

Chapter 9

It had been two years since the murder of Dr Goldsmith. Another police file had been opened and closed as potential leads dried up, then everything was put in the unsolved cupboard. No knocks on the door, no questions asked, his solid alibi ready for such an emergency, the Timestopper had done it again.

Since that awful night, John had only just managed to conceal his fears and nightmares on the gruesome deed he had done, all arranged to simply cover his tracks and to prove a point. His marriage had long gone, his old job a distant memory but most of all, his displeasure of how he had changed as a man. In the early days, he wouldn't allow anything to come before his so-called "talent". He wanted to prove it to himself, as well as the world, but had no idea of the mental consequences, the anguish, the physicality or indeed, how his whole mind-set had changed.

During the long spell since the murder, he had to force himself to move on, he had no other choice and no one could know anything at all about his past. No one could be told and he couldn't confide in anyone either, he simply knew he would have to let the past go, lock the door and put it behind him. His gift had proved little use or worth, only to torture and torment him throughout the whole process, it had let him down and it couldn't be trusted anymore.

John had banished his thoughts and feelings to the darkest part of his mind, living a lie, but at least now, he was beginning to reap the rewards, and at least have some kind of normality. He was at last, thinking ahead with good friends around him and finding a new job, the memories of the past, were veiled. He was too scared to even attempt the Timestop process like before, and wasn't about to even try.

He loved his new lifestyle, his new way of life. He felt much more of his old self, joking and laughing, socialising with work colleagues, and above all, with his new girlfriend Anna. A work friend had introduced John to Anna at a party, and they instantly hit it off. Raised in the same area and went to the same school, although she was four years younger. A beautiful girl who had just the desired influence on John that he wanted, calming him, trusting him, and being considerate towards him, it could only make for a very special relationship. His life was beginning to take shape, but that grim darkness would always lurk in the back of his mind, behind a huge protective wall he had built for himself, holding back the dark secrets, unpleasant memories and scars. Yet, he knew he had to continue to fight the thoughts, the nightmares, and the despair, if he didn't want mental damage to mess up his life again.

"Right... yes... I know... Yes... Yes..." John had the

phone to his ear with Anna on the other end of the line. "Yes, I know I'm late Anna. If you get off the phone, I may be able to finish getting ready and then I can pick you up."

As usual, the conversation ended in laughter and soon John was on his way to meet up with Anna for her birthday party treat. She didn't know, but he had organised a surprise birthday party for her at her favourite restaurant with some very close friends. She thought they were going to see a movie, but John explained there wasn't anything good showing at the local cinema, so he thought it better to go for a nice dinner. When they arrived at the restaurant, she was overjoyed with the surprise and friends she hadn't seen for a while, she was so happy. The night was a total success, John and his friend Tom, went to the downstairs bar to pay the bill.

"I'm just nipping to the loo mate." Tom made off in the direction of the toilets. John was unaware of the woman behind him who gave him a sharp poke in the back, when he turned around it was Lilly. *"Oh god!"* he thought.

"Hi John, my dearest ex. I thought that was you." Lilly appeared to be very drunk, very unsteady, and slurring her words. She was loud, and with a group of people he didn't recognise, not Lilly's usual acquaintances and very dodgy looking, not pleasant at all he thought, this wasn't like her.

"How's the disappearing act going, John?" She asked in a provocative loud manner. He knew he had to remain calm, hoping she didn't blurt out the true story.
"I'm doing okay Lilly, my treatment is working, and yes, you will be glad to hear, you were right it was all in my mind" Just then to Johns relief, Tom came back and commented on Lilly,
"Well hello there!" John immediately introduced Lilly as his ex-wife. Tom was staring at her, not a head turner as she used to be, but more an embarrassing drunk.

"Well, we must be off Lilly, was nice seeing you."
John said unnervingly and started to walk away.

 As he was walking away, Lilly shouted, "You
showed someone that time thing, didn't you? that
bleeding quack… Goldstein or Goldmine or
whatever his name was, you showed him and he
believed you, didn't you John?" Tom was watching
John waiting for his reply.

There was a long silence and John replied, "Yeah, I
did, but he told me it was all in my mind. Anyway,
that was ages ago and I'm okay now."

"Did you know he's dead?" she slurred, "Murdered
in his own garden apparently."

"I didn't actually, but thanks for the information."
He shouted as both Tom and he went around the
corner and upstairs, back to their party.

Tom immediately revealed the chance meeting with Lilly to the rest of the group, and what she had said. John's mind was sharp, and he quickly stepped in with a retort, saying she was just twisted with bitterness about their divorce and how she couldn't handle his past problems. Fortunately, on their meeting, John had explained to Anna about his ex-wife and his previous history, excluding his time stopping days, so the little scene at the restaurant was explained away exactly as he wanted. The last part of the conversation with Lilly made John very nervous in fact, he hadn't felt that way for a long time, feeling, he was being scrutinised and cornered. He knew he couldn't let this get the better of him. He needed to forget about what had just happened and see it as a one off and it would never happen again. Lilly knew nothing, well, at least he hoped so.

For several weeks after the meeting, John was feeling very nervous, very anxious. He kept asking himself, was Lilly aware of what has happened over the past few years and if so, what the hell did she know? what would she do about it? who would even believe her? He was trying to convince himself that everything was okay. It was troubling him a great deal; he was starting to notice weird things. He was getting more and more wrong number calls on his mobile, and he had received two letters with the correct address, but the wrong name. Last week he was in the local market, which was very busy, and had his wallet lifted by a pick pocket. Was all this a co-incidence? or was it indeed connected with bloody Lilly? His mind was playing tricks with him again, he was feeling paranoid. *"Jesus,"* he thought, *"I'm not going down that route again, not now."*

It took a good few weeks for John to get to grip with everything that was going on and he was convinced it was just him and his insecurities getting the best of him. Then, one night, he was working at home on a project for a new client, it was late, and he was so tired. The house phone broke the silence with a loud ring, he just thought bugger it, they can call back, and then the machine scratched out his answer phone message "...after the tone etc" A familiar drunken voice spoke,

"Hi my favourite divorcee. I know your fucking in, so pick up the phone. I have a deal for you." John flew across the room and answered,

"What the bloody hell do you want Lilly? Don't you know what time it is?"

"Fuck off John, and listen to what I've got to say. I have a new friend who knows all about you and the golden Jew, Goldsmith."

"What about him Lilly? That's not new. You introduced him to me if you remember, to get some treatment, so what's new?"

A long paused ensued then, "His death, that's what's new. I know you did it, with your ability as you used to call it, the thing you used to try and tell me about. Well the only difference now my dearest, is my new friend also had Mr Goldsmith as an acquaintance and he confirmed your secret talent to him."

John waited a while, "This is all bollocks, I don't know who your new mate is, or what he knows but it's all shite..."

Lilly stopped him mid-sentence, "JOHN, HE'S A FUCKIN REPORTER." She shouted down the phone. After another long silence, she continued, "It's very simple John and we have it all figured out. We want some dosh from you, or everything we know is going to the police. Have I got you attention now?"

"Lilly, listen to me very closely and listen good. You and your hack reporter have got fucking nothing and you know what you and your reporter are gonna get, fuck all, zilch, zero, not a penny, so fuck off and do what you want." There was a cold silence as he hung up.

John's brow was sweating profusely as he looked at himself in the mirror. *"What the fuck do I do now and who was this fucking reporter bloke she's talking about?* He needed a plan, and bloody quick. One thing he did know, it might be the case that Lilly had slipped into society circles, but she was still the same inside. All the years he had known her, she never gave up on anything, and she certainly wouldn't give up this time, she had more bitterness, scores to settle, and money to be made from it.

His mind flowed with possibilities of how to get out of this but he kept coming up with nothing. Perhaps the only way was the Goldsmith way, the Timestopper way? But there was someone else involved now. Maybe he could wait it out as they couldn't prove anything. It's not as if they could make him go into Timestop mode. "I would just deny it, and any court would think they were the crazy ones". He thought this was the only option he had now, and they had nothing.

John sat at the bar in his local, reading the local rag and having a quiet pint, when the seat next to him was taken up by a guy he had never seen in the pub before, he gestured to John, he nodded. Sitting silently delving into the newspaper John's reading was interrupted by the guest,

"Can't believe everything you read, can you?" The stranger said.

"No, you can't." John said nervously.

"I read the other day, about a bloke who said he could stop time, who the hell could do that? What will they print next?" John ignored the man and started to fold the paper away, he was about to leave when the stranger said,

"John, we need to talk mate."

The bars only regulars were few and looking around uneasily, John replied, "Who the fuck are you?"

Laughing he said, "I'm your mate John. Let's go around the corner and talk, it may be in both our best interests." They moved around into the corner of the room and sat down at a table.

The stranger spoke, staring intently, "Listen here, Mr. high and mighty McAndrew, I know what you can do, also who you've proved it too and what it resulted in.? All we want is a little bit of security money, that's all. I'm sure you'll agree it's better than prison. It's not a nice place Mr McAndrew not a nice place at all. Oh, by the way, my name is Jimmy

Conran, you may have heard of me in the local press, a reporter of considerable attributes."

John looked carefully around the room, no one was listening to them, "Listen here you piece of shit, neither you or Lilly know fuck all, nothing that could incriminate me in any way, so I'll tell you what I told her, fuck off, and do what you have to as you will be the ones who look stupid in front of the police or magistrate, you've got fuck all. You've got no physical evidence that they would be interested in, only conjecture".

"Do you really think that? Do you think we would make this move without any evidence? Well you are wrong. I can put you at the scene of the first supermarket robbery. Once the police know what we know, they will link it to all the other crimes. Is it worth the gamble John?"

John rose from the chair, he really wanted to kill this man for messing with his life, he knew they must have something. He stood for a while and whispered in the man's ear, "Fuck off, and try it MATE!" with that he walked back to the bar ordered another pint and sat with his newspaper. Jimmy left by the rear door but looked over at John one last time before walking out of the door.

Chapter 10

The Old Mare public house was jumping, full of smoke and stale beer, wafted around the room. Saturday night was live music night, local scallies, and drug dealers were in abundance flogging their wares to unsuspecting juveniles. The landlord was aware of what was happening in his pub but past caring. Times were hard, he didn't give a shit about its clientele, providing they made the tills rattle, that's all he wanted. In his usual corner was Jimmy Conran, doing deals, selling stories or whatever he could for a fast buck. Jimmy was never the brightest button in the box, how he survived was a mystery. He'd never had a decent story for years.

The crowd's noise was broken by a burly man, silence descended across the crowded space, they all knew who he was. Walking straight over to Jimmy, a pint was quickly served to his table. DC Tom Myers certainly had Jimmy's attention as the bar slowly returned to its normal volume.

"Now then James, any joy? Have you and your new friend had any luck with our little project?" "No Tom. I said what you told me, and he didn't bat an eyelid. He's a clever shit, says it's all circumstantial."

Heads turned as a sudden burst of energy with a raised voice from the DC got their attention, "Look your stupid bastard, what did I tell you? I've got the footage that puts him right where I need him. I searched for fuckin hours through that shit tape, back and bloody forward, but I've got it. One minute he's standing with a bag outside the shop and in the next very small fraction of a second, he's bloody moved to a different spot, just a slight movement, which says to me something happened in that time and with the time stop story, as tall as it is, what you've told me, and she confirmed it. Come on, don't you get it you dozy shit?"

"Yeah, sure I do, but what now?"

"Look Jimmy, I didn't say this would be easy to prove, but given to a boffin squad, they could sort it out no problem and he could be banged away, that's what we've got to sell to him, and if anything else is linked to him, they'll through away the friggin key, we just need to put the frighteners on. He's not the sort to go to the nick, he's never been in trouble before. He would shit himself if it got to that. No, he'll pay up I know he will, then after we get the money, he's shopped. Yeah, he'll bleat on about bribery but no one would believe it, a fine serving officer like me." he laughed out loudly, "If he's done all those unsolved robberies this way, you're talking big bucks' mate."

There was a break in the deep conversation. "So, shouldn't you go and see him?" said Jimmy, "Tell him what we've got on him?"

"Hello!!" DC Myers said sarcastically, "I tell you what, you dumb shit. Why don't I go and say to him? Hello Mr McAndrew, I am DC Myers and I am a member of the local police force wanting bribery money for withholding evidence, you stupid bastard." He took a breath before continuing, "No, our next step is, I've got a mate in tech operations and, I know he can keep his gob shut for a few bob, if he can enhance the footage, then you go with the disk and show the sneaky bastard what we've got, tell him we mean business, if he coughs up with the money he's in the clear to enjoy some of his ill-gotten gains. If not, he's in the clink, got it?"

"Yeah, Tom. That sounds good but can I put anything to print yet, I'm desperate for a good story?"

Tom stared at him and shook his head, "No! you stupid fucking bastard."

Silence followed the officer out of the pub again, with one or two fingered gestures and daring muffled jeers. He got into his car and from outside, he could hear the noise level increase to normal. Tom's thoughts were of a nice little pension pot, so he reviewed his plan. "Right that's sorted, I'll get that dozy shit to do the donkey work, cut them both off, and then reap the rewards. Once I've got the dosh, McAndrew's fuckin nicked. Go to print, what a fuckin prick." He turned the key to start the car and with a cheesy grin on his face, drove away.

"Welcome to the Hundley Hotel and Spa, can I take a reservation name please?"

"Yes, its McAndrew."

"Okay, Sir, I'll not be a moment." The receptionist quickly put all that was needed for John and Anna into a folded card and asked the porter to attend to their luggage.

With a welcoming smile, the receptionist advised them, "Room 326, straight along the corridor and first right and up the stairs, or there is a lift if you prefer, have a pleasant stay with us."

On arrival in their room, they both spread eagled on the king size bed. It had been a long journey, but they were both pleased to be starting this first holiday together.

"Fancy a drink in the bar Anna?"

"Yeah, okay but I'm tired, I'll meet you down there if that's okay? I'll just freshen up a little."

"Okay darling, see you soon."

John made his way to the coral cocktail bar and lounge, "Whiskey on the rocks and a gin and tonic please." Sat at the bar, John gazed at the mirrored back fitting of the bar only to give a small gasp when hovering around the room he saw that bloody reporter, Conran. Peering into every corner, checking people out, then he eventually spied John and made his way over.

"Hello my mate, fancy meeting you hear."

John turned him by the collar, "You bastard, you followed us. You better not have brought that drunken tart with you."

"Calm down, I'm on my own, just thought I would get a nice bit of R & R following all the hard work

I've been doing. Well it's so nice to see you again, what a small world it is."

John spouted after seeing Anna coming down the stairs whispering to Jimmy, "Fuck Off."

Anna approached while the Jimmy departed into the farthest part of the lounge. Shrugging her shoulders, "And who...?" She quizzed.

"A client from last year. He's local apparently, I didn't even know he lived around here."

"John, I know we're on a bit of a jolly, but if you two need to talk..."

He interrupted her, "No darling."

"Well, I was about to say, I'll have this one with you and I'll go up, I am so tired, have a bit of a chin wag with your friend if you want."

"We'll see, he's not that important."

Anna advanced up the stairs, and once around the corner, John rushed over to Conran who was patiently waiting, "You stupid git, what do you want?"

"If I didn't know better, more threats likely."

"Listen, you shit bag hack, if all this doesn't stop, it will be me going to the police."

John was about to continue his onslaught into Jimmy when he was stopped by Jimmy held his hand up, "Shut the fuck up. I have another contact John, and he's got footage which proves the time thing is you. You moved. The one thing you didn't think of and you didn't get it right, so who's the dumb shit now."

John sat stunned at what had just been reported, god he was right, he never thought about the final position when I came out of it, *"Oh god, for fucks sake."* He thought.

"Obviously, by your lack of response, I think I may just have your attention. Okay, listen up. This is the deal, we want two hundred thousand pounds or all of this goes to the police and leaked into the press, as an insurance policy."

"How the fuck can I get that sort of money? I could never raise that sort of cash."

"See John. we know you've done banks before and

doing a couple more wouldn't hurt then your job is done. That's the deal, and you've got two weeks to sort it or be prepared for the knock on the door."

John pondered, "So, let's say I didn't go along with it, you'll end up with sod all anyway, so what's the point?"

"Rewards my mate, rewards, that's the point. They still stand for the jobs you've pulled, and all of them jobs will be proven. The police would love it, crime figures etcetera, etcetera, and the money wouldn't be close to our chosen sum but a very tidy bundle, nevertheless. Just remember though, two weeks, or off you go for a long time."

"Jimmy, this will never work, the evidence is too weak, so please yourself and oh, Jimmy, just for the record, I'm not your fucking mate. Got it!"

DC Tom Myers phone lit up by his bed, "Dumb shit" lit up on his caller screen. He quietly answered the call. "It's done mate." was the reply.

"Okay, now, we'll wait." He answered, then hung up and went back to sleep.

═══════════════════════════════

The door bell sounded at Johns home, it sounded again, and again, as if there was some sort of emergency requirement for him to attend.

"All right, all right." he shouted at the closed and locked front door, "Wait a bloody minute."

John unlocked the front door and opened it but a sudden pain ran through his chest, which sent him stumbling backward and over the edge of the sofa. Reeling in agony from the pain that surged through his body was tremendous, like a heart attack. Following unrelenting pain, he eventually passed out.

When he awoke, to his relief he hadn't been shot or injured and felt reasonably okay. What the hell was going on? He looked at his wrists which were firmly held firm with handcuffs, his ankles were trussed up like a turkey. He looked around, but no one was in sight and he sensed someone was in the house but he didn't know what to expect. Had he been rumbled after all this time? He didn't think so.

He gave a shout, "Hello, hello, who the hell are you and what do you want?"

No reply.

The house was eerily quiet, when suddenly a guy appeared from the kitchen, slurping coffee. He was dishevelled and scruffy, but didn't seem aggressive.

"What do you want?" said John. "I've got no money in the house, but you can take anything you see." The guy just stared at him, a shiny bald head was reflecting from the lights and his bright blue eyes were looking right through him.

"What the fuck do you want?"

"Now, now, John. Don't get nasty." said the stranger. *"He knows my name, who the fuck is he?"*

"I know you're a bit confused John, but don't get too scared just yet, I am not going to hurt or rob you, we just need to talk."

"I've got nothing to say to you, you bastard, you nearly killed me." John was stopped mid-sentence by the man.

"John if I wanted to kill you, I guarantee, you would be cold by now, so shut the fuck up and listen, listen very, very carefully. I handcuffed you because what I am about to tell you, you may choose not to like or believe, and because you're a little bit bigger than me, I thought it was wise. Oh, I forgot to mention, don't try the time halt thing because it won't work." he suddenly turned right into Johns face, "Do you know why it won't work John?"

"No, I don't" John said in amazement and fear at the strangers statement.

"It's because I can do it to. Yeah, John. There's not only you with this fuckin thing."

After releasing the breath, he didn't know he had been holding, John relaxed a little and the stranger continued talking, "Now, I bet your wondering loads of things, aren't you? Well, I can only tell you a few answers, but what I will say is today is the day when your life changes John, no more fuckin about. You can't frig off the government, yeah, I said the government with a capital G."

John stared in disbelief from what he was saying, "Who and what are you? some sort of James Bond, or agent?"

"Don't be so fucking stupid McAndrew. Do I look like James Bond? That's all in fiction and books, this is the real world my boy, and trust me, some of it you won't like. You belong to us now John, my department, address of which is HM UK."

A long pause followed, only spoiled by sips of brewed coffee. He announced "You have been conscripted, as they used to call it. You will hone your skills and they will be used for the things we want, your country wants, got it? Not just robbing shops and killing doctors, we are the real deal. You don't have a life now, you won't see any of your friends or acquaintances again, your sole purpose in life is to assist and participate with your government in the pursuit of security for this country. Am I going to fast with this? Do you understand what I am saying? I'm going to release you from the cuffs now, but believe me, if you try anything, I press this button and there will be more people in here, faster than a tube at rush hour."

John looked terrified and nodded. "Am I being arrested?"

"No, you're not being arrested, your being hired, your ours now. Steady now." he turned towards John and released him from his shackles.

"Putting the cup down." the stranger announced, "Today John, is the start of your new life. You will be reborn into the darker side of our country, our hidden world. Just get you coat; you don't need anything else, and by the way, your mobile and house phones don't work so don't bother trying them. Just go along with it, and don't worry about the pain from before. I promise, it will go away. Forty thousand volts does hurt for a little while you know."

Chapter 11

Today was his seventh week in training, in captivity he called it. He was missing his basic rights, needs, friends, family, good times, and his old life. He was missing all of this terribly and his girlfriend, now ex-girlfriend, Anna. What she must be thinking, He had just disappeared, without saying a word, too anyone. They told him the department had laid a false trail with the police, he was accused of embezzlement and fraud. This was to be handled by the serious crime squad as it was confirmed that he had fled the country. Unknown to the Police, this along with all the files, and identities on the old John McAndrew had been, unexplainably destroyed. A new identity was created for him, all new documents, birth certs etcetera. Some facial work had been completed, giving John a totally different profile than before, yet he remained John McAndrew, just born on a different date.

His training was relentless, albeit mental, all done to benefit his ability, this was their intention, to have a finely tuned operative ready for any sort of action. No criminal record and perfectly innocent. In the early weeks, he had thought of escaping this predicament, there weren't any guards or security and it would have been so easy but, where could he go? or where could he hide? they knew they had him and if he gave these people too much trouble, he would be gone for good, as quick as his old identity. Johns only hope was to wait it out to see what they were about and then plan his next move.

He had been told just a few things about the section, how secret it was, where it was in the security ladder and most of all, the importance and what it meant to the security of the country. He found out that the guy who came to his house, was a selection commander named Roper, his department brief was purely to source out Timestoppers like John. Using police un-solved records and associated press stories that couldn't be explained and that was their route to John. The official information the police had on unexplained crimes that John had instigated were swiftly removed from all records and were stored in his personnel file as an insurance policy for future use. They were a mystifying group of operatives and they could simply disappear into the world that they created very easily, re-appearing with their own set of rules, nothing was beyond their reach and worryingly, every contact was expendable.

When John was captured, he remembered Roper mentioning John wasn't the only Timestopper, and that had intrigued him. If that were the case, where were the others. He was in a special military area just outside the capital and he was not allowed any kind of contact with anyone, the exception being his tutors, and someone called Grenville. He doubted that this was his real name, and his behaviour suggested he was definitely in charge. He had been in the Parachute Regiment and had served all over the world in many conflicts. He even had gallantry medals, awards and stood no nonsense from anyone, he seemed a very tough cookie. John felt Grenville had taken an instant dislike to him, not being Army, just a civilian or perhaps his dislikes were linked to Johns abilities. Maybe, Grenville couldn't understand them, because he was brought up Old School, kill, or be killed. John knew he had to be very wary of this one.

When the training ended, which seemed like months. He could Timestop for over 45mins and was told by the doctors and tutors, that this will get better with practice and time. They supplied him with drugs to counteract any side effects which, surprisingly, did work, unlike the old days of self-medication.

John had no reason to trust any of the team, trust wasn't part of this new world and you relied on your own metal, suspicion of them being paramount, thoughts of the guarded secrets they must have, and the darkness of the unknown, made a very nervous, and dangerous thinking for John. A knock at the door and John was greeted by Roper who invited John to a briefing to discuss the "Settlement and Deployment" of Mr John McAndrew. All so very posh, he thought as he headed to the briefing room.

Before him sat, Roper, Grenville and four uniformed personnel, who were not named, John sat down at the end of the table and Roper began. He said that John had done very well in his training and now needed to move on to the next level. Reading from a prepared script he commenced. "We will secure you in a position within the local community which will not hinder your work with this department. Employment with a Financial Agency has been organised as a Freelance Advisor. We know in your past life, you were very good at this type of career, hence the role.

You will be expected to blend in and socialise with your work colleagues and neighbours, gaining trust, friendship and possible acquittances. This cover must be maintained McAndrew, for your sake, not ours, do you understand." John nodded in agreement.

"All costs will be provided by us for living arrangements, you will be provided with a vehicle, unlimited credit card and bank details at the end of this meeting. Okay, we have a property in mind which will serve our purposes and you will be moved there as soon as possible. Your work commitments are flexible and as far as your employer is concerned, they will be expecting you to be working from home most of the time, this will allow your cover, we will provide any false leads/documents that you may need to operate in the pretence of your job, but they do expect to see you every now and then, okay?" John nodded again. he thought to himself, *"I could live with this."*

"The main objective John, is to blend in and you must make it real. There must be no suspicions at all. You must never use your skills for your own benefit or enjoyment and if your cover is revealed..."
Grenville butted in and joined the conversation "If you blow it and this department is compromised, I will personally issue a termination order." Looking at Grenville, Roper shook his head and continued,

"Do you understand all that has been discussed today Mr McAndrew?"

"Yes, Yes, I do."

"Any questions?"

"No, Thank you."

John left the room with muffled groans from Grenville and the words "termination order" ringing through his head.

The next day, John followed the directions he had been given, finding the road to Stadley Cottage, a single-track road that went for nearly half a mile, finally revealing a beautiful chocolate box cottage, with flowers up the outside and thatched roof. "Very nice." he thought to himself out loud, "Looks okay so far." Stopping on the gravel drive. He entered the property, "Oh yeah, this is the business." It exceeded all of Johns expectations, which gave him a warmness that was satisfying, he felt he had finally reached some sort of milestone.

That night, he stood by the log fire pondering, *"I start my new job tomorrow. I hope I can blend in well."* His mind was jumping around the Grand Plan when reality prevailed, *"Come on John, get your act together."* He had already checked out the area and his local was a stone's throw away from the house. *"Well come on McAndrew, it's time to meet some neighbours."* So, the government agent slash financial advisor went off in search of friends and maybe romance.

Soon after his Settlement and Deployment, John received a text to collect a parcel from the local rail station property boxes, a code was given for the lock, and inside was a large brown envelope.

John sat in his car with the large brown envelope on the passenger seat, wondering what this was all about. He headed back to his house and ripped open the envelope, he was so excited and at the same time very nervous. It was his first mission orders. The mission statement said, he was to go to a place called Suceava, in Romania. All the required documents were in the envelope, hotel reservations, flight tickets, a mobile phone, contact telephone numbers, and a wedge of local money. Other than that, there were no exact details, but all of this was all happening tomorrow and he'd be leaving from Heathrow.

Chapter 12

The rain was pouring from the heavens when John touched down at Suceava airport. He looked out at the airport surroundings and it was a bleak and dreary place with armed police dotted around the buildings, the one hundred or so passengers disembarked very quickly. Standing in the security queue, John was very nervous and a security officer glared at him for what seemed like ages.

"You here on holiday or business?" Johns brief was a businessman which he quickly confirmed.

An unhealthy silence began, a huge amount of words were spoken to the adjacent security guard who, although listening to his partner, stared and weighed up John.

"Okay, have a good stay sir." John could feel the

sweat running down his back, he thought to himself, *"I'm shite at this."* He quickly headed to the airport concourse for a taxi, looking around nervously, he managed to hail a cab, throwing his bag in the back and jumped in wiping the perspiration from his brow.

"The Continental Hotel please." The cab immediately drove off.

A few minutes passed and the driver asked, "You here on business?"

"Yeah." He replied, "Just a few days."

Johns nerves were beginning to show. "You Mr McAndrew?"

"Yes, yes, I am."

"I have a message for you. A friendly person will ask to meet with you in the hotel tonight, you must attend, okay?"

John didn't reply to the driver as he was too gobsmacked. The taxi pulled up and John checked into his temporary new home....

Later that night, lying on the bed in his very comfortable room, a drink in hand, he reviewed what was happening to him, and his life. What would his old friends have made of all this? His attention was diverted when the phone rang, and reception told him a guest was waiting for him in the lounge. "Okay, I'll be down soon, he responded before putting the phone back on the receiver.

Wondering who this could be, John finished his drink then headed down to the lounge, walking in, a slim attractive blonde girl approached him, "Mr McAndrew?"

"Yes."

"Come with me please." She led him to a more quiet and intimate part of the lounge.

"Please sit-down John, my name is Catina, and I am your Romanian contact and a worker within your project. I can help you in many ways with anything you require, but first, I will discuss why you are here, and what is expected from you." She was quite firm in her delivery of the terms. She continued, "There will be no failures, everything that is being asked of you, WILL happen. Do you understand?" He nodded.

"Now, place some money on the table please, about one thousand Romanian Leu should do. Now let me explain a few things, for security reasons the other people in this lounge and the hotel must assume you are buying me for tonight, a sex worker I think you would call it. So, after our meeting we will both leave, and go to your room. This is normal in Romania and no one watching us would suspect anything."

John grinned, "Sounds good to me."

She stared at him and said, "Just listen, all you have to do for now is occasionally smile and don't even dream about what you think may happen with us. It's a cover story, period." She continued in her matter of fact voice. "I have no doubt, that you must have known about the Russian and Ukraine conflicts over the past few years. But not all you hear, is the truth. A very strong bond has developed between the military leaders, which we have on good authority, could lead to tension within Europe. We need some vital documents from the Ukrainian embassy, which only you have the skills to obtain." She paused for a moment to smile and force a laugh, while drinking her martini.

"I would be lying to you if I said this wasn't dangerous. Our people will get you where you need to be, then all you must do is confiscate some papers and remove some special articles, do you understand?"

Again, John nodded.

"I can tell you Mr McAndrew, when your task is complete, it should eliminate the threat of an invasion that the Ukrainian forces have planned for many months. If allowed, their actions would see them take control of Poland, and of course, supported by Russia. More importantly, we are asking you to steal some items which relate to some codes that the Ukrainians have been given, by the Russian military, which, if used, would see a missile strike from Russia to strategic targets in Poland to assist in the invasion, these codes must be obtained and secured. Is everything clear John am I going to fast? If so, just say."

He sat stunned of what he had been told but still she continued as if it was never-ending, "The repercussions of this, without our intervention would be outright war in Europe."
"Oh, Holy Jesus." John didn't doubt his skills and he knew he could complete a time stop no problem, but he certainly wasn't an MI5 agent by a long way.

He looked at her very attractive face, her deep brown eyes were fixed, as if all this information was normal, and it happened every day in her life. She looked at him, waiting for a reply, John said he understood.

Smiling she stood up and announced, "You have helped my country, and my people, I am truly grateful. Now, let's go to your room." That was the best news John had heard all night, although he knew nothing would come of it. She was dedicated to the cause, which was slightly different to Johns.

The next morning, John woke with a head full of memories, disappointedly minus Catina, who, as promised had left his room that night after completing a few texts, doing the crossword and a quick gin and tonic. In fact, no words were spoken between them in the room, which, although John thought was weird, gave much needed time to digest all that she had spoken earlier. She had been kind enough to leave a small note, saying, *"Thank you for all your help, myself and my country will be forever in your debt."* signed Catina and a phone number. His thoughts were shattered by a sudden loud buzz coming from the mobile he was supplied with. He picked it up and it read, A nice suit, shirt and tie, lobby one hour...

John quickly got ready as instructed and then poured himself a large stiff drink. The bloody mobile screeched again, he grabbed the phone, nerves shattered once more, he had another text and a picture downloading. The text informed John that they were downstairs, but no rush and memorise the picture and then destroy the phone. The picture eventually downloaded, and it was an image of three matchbox sized coloured boxes, one red, one blue dot, and one yellow triangles. He didn't understand, but what was new! John made his way down to the hotel lobby and was met by a delegation of three men.

"We're going to a rendezvous point to brief you of the main plan, your specific role, is this okay?" John nodded in agreement.

"After that, we'll drive to the Ukrainian embassy." nothing else was said, not even names.

They arrived at a back-street office complex about twenty minutes away and then they made their way inside but the place was deserted. A plan was produced, and placed on the table in front of them.

"John, this is the part of the embassy we will be compromising." he pointed to a room in the centre of the plan. "Our cover, is the embassy staff, along with the British Ambassador are having an event in the main hall for the local business community; and we represent the possible business available in the UK. We are there to consult and help if they are interested and as you can imagine, we will not be allowed anywhere else in the building. As you can imagine, it is heavily guarded and security systems are in place and this is where you come in. You will stop time, then walk to the security office and take a set of keys marked "Cleaners Cupboard."

This was a lot of information for John to take in but he felt there was more to come. And, he was right, "On this bunch of keys, there will be a key for the safe in the private office of the High Commissionaire. You will go there, open the safe, and look for the files marked, "Summer Sun." These will be removed. In the rear of the safe, is a compartment for high security items and it has a digital lock with a code, but you must remember this." John studied the code and gave the man the piece of paper back.

"In the secure box, you will find a further box containing twenty different small boxes and the colours you received by text today, must be the ones removed. Leave everything as it was and then move back to here, start time again and continue with the event. Within an hour of your return, the four of us will leave by the main entrance, a doorman will usher us to a waiting car, and you will be dropped at the airport.

All your belongings will be in the boot of the car and your flight back to London will be shortly after your arrival at airport. You will keep the packages in your briefcase. If your stopped and asked what they are, tell them they are samples for a product you are exporting but don't worry, they won't have a clue what you really have. On arrival in London, you will be contacted for collection, but above all, don't worry. With your abilities, no one will be aware that anything has been taken for about a week. John was white and sweating, he was trying to remain calm, which they noticed.

"Don't worry, if anyone asks, we'll just say you've had some bad food. When all this is over, you will have played a major part in saving so many lives, so stay cool."

"Hello Ambassador, may I introduce…" the introductions disappeared into an audible blur, with the odd head nod, but nerves were playing a big part.

Hello, and how do you do? Thank you for attending our little event, which may be lucrative to all, including the UK business market."
"Let's hope so, Mr Ambassador." and with that over, the ambassador was ushered to other waiting people.

John stood motionless trying to gather his thoughts.
"Okay, mate. Let's do this." said one of the group.
John made his way to a corner of the room and
stopped time and as always, the place was quiet, but
it was much easier for him now. Quickly getting
gloved, he located his quarry, got the keys and
headed for the safe. John's hands were trembling,
but it opened as expected and the documents he
need, were laying right on the top, that was lucky.
He pushed aside some other stuff to reveal the digital
safe. He wiped away the sweat that was running into
his eyes and running down his cheeks. He began
entering the code, but nothing happened, nothing.
"Shit, that wasn't it." He said to himself, then
nervously, he tried again. The heavy locks slid back
to reveal the box of boxes, he remembered these no
problem, so he put the ones he needed in his pocket,
locked all of the safes, the doors, and returned to the
room which remained in perfect silence. He looked
at his watch and fifteen minutes had passed. Back in
the corner of the room, he started time again and the

background music started up as if nothing had happened, the ambient talking noise returned back to normal.

The group looked inquisitively at him, he nodded, "It's done." smiles all round. The waiter brought four more drinks and they all looked at each other. "Ah, why the hell not." Drinks down, they headed for the door knowing now it was up to someone else now, to carry on with this mission, they had done their part in a very large jigsaw, All the men in the group said, "Goodbye."

Sitting in executive class on the way home, John considered his adventure and for him it was exciting, heart stopping, and exhilarating all in one. It wasn't as difficult as he thought it would be, but he knew, he was just a minor part of a very big machine, everything had been designed, planned, and laid out as intended. Although he knew his department would give him up in a heartbeat, or deny even knowing him if they needed too. The people he worked with, were all dispensable pawns in a game. He wondered if they all were safe and would he ever know. A loud bump signalled the return to his native soil.

The porter took John up to his temporary home, hotel room 1126. "This is your room sir."
"Thank you." John replied and gave him a few quid. The porter hesitated for a while, as if to say the tip wasn't sufficient.
"I believe you have a package for me sir?"
"Package? No, I am afraid not, you must be mistaken. what sort of package?"
"It's okay sir," backing out of the room. "Sorry, I apologise. It was my error, please have a good night."

John lay on his bed going through everything that had happened, including the awkward conversation with the porter. "surely not," he thought, "give the special codes to a hotel porter? How the hell do I know who he is? He may be with the other side." querying himself, wondering if he had made the right choice. "Ah, what the hell. I'm so tired it's been a long day." His thoughts hauled him off to slumber, drifting away with Catina heavily on his mind.

John awoke in a frightened nightmare state, only to find Grenville and a large security guy leaning over his bed.

Grenville lent over and whispered quietly, "Listen shit face, you don't know how lucky you were tonight. That porter, obviously of our team, could have quite easily killed you for not complying, your stupid bastard."

John stuttered "I just wanted to make sure the right person got the goods."

"Just remember this. You haven't got a clue about this organisation, and who is in it, everyone we have working for us, is a potential killer. It's just your little softy Timestopper lot, who think they are the bees knees who think they can get away with everything because of what they can do. What a load of bullshit."

John was beginning to feel nervous in the presence

of Grenville and the other guy. Grenville wasn't finished with him yet though. "Give me the fucking stuff now and don't think you've heard the last of this, you dumb shit." The packages were handed over and they finally left. John approached the familiar bathroom mirror, looking at his worried and tired face and thought, *"I guess I'm back to square one then."*

Chapter 13

A few years had passed since John had been deployed by the department. He successfully completed many missions, some small and some very important to do with the security of the country. His life was at last, beginning to settle and become normal, to a certain extent. He had acquaintances and work friendships, in fact, it was just like his previous life, but all generated by the organization. His relationship had blossomed with a girl from the finance agency, Lauren, who was a sweet, quiet, and loving girl. She would stay with John on some occasions or at weekends. She never quizzed John of his missing days or long stayovers, and what he did on his days off, she presumed it was something to do with his work.

They had a good group of fun-loving friends who were always up for a laugh. He had gained most trust in one colleague, a guy called Matt, who used to be in the forces, eventually settling down to civilian life and a boring selling career. His girlfriend, Julia, also knew Lauren from school, so they all made a perfect foursome. John felt he could trust Matt, but not to the point where he would reveal all. Matt often asked John about his past and where he was born, had he been married etcetera, etcetera and at first, this worried John. Should he say the truth or would it matter? but in the end, he thought it best to stick with his cover identity as supplied, which didn't sit comfortably with him and he hated lying.

The house phone rang, it was Lauren, "Hey, darling. I've got a surprise for you."

"Hey, love. You have a surprise for me? What's that then?"

"How do you fancy a weekend foursome for your birthday next month?"

"That sounds great."

"Are you up for it?"

"Ah thanks, Lauren, that would be brilliant, you're a

gem. Where we off too then?"

John's heart sank as, she revealed she was taking him to his old stamping ground and his previous home area.

The phone went quiet, "Well, what do you say? There's a festival on and I've booked the hotel for the four of us, it will be great."

"Sounds good." he said nervously.

"Are you sure?" she replied, "You don't sound too happy about it?"

"It's just, I need to check my diary."

"Don't worry, I checked it last night when I was at yours, and there's nothing in there until the Tuesday after."

John blurted out the only thing he could say, "Okay, brilliant, thanks a lot." With that, they said their goodbyes.

"Shit, Shit, Shit." pacing the room, "What the hell do I do now?"

John realised this was his new life now, and he felt certain nobody would recognise him from years ago.

To reassure himself he searched a drawer in his desk and found his memory stick with pictures from his past on. Quickly, he attached it to the computer and was shocked to see the vast difference of how he looked then in comparison to now. His eyes glanced at a picture of Lilly, who he loved so much, and always felt guilty for their breakup. If only she'd have believed him. He figured, at least the past doesn't look so scary, and John was convinced he could get away with this little jaunt and his mood began to improve.

The phone was ringing continuously, "Okay, I'm coming," John shouted as he ran from the bathroom dripping wet from the shower. He picked up the phone, "HAPPY BIRTHDAY TO YOU, HAPPY BIRTHDAY TO YOU, HAPPY BIRTHDAY DEAR JOHN, HAPPY BIRTHDAY TO YOU." Loads of laughter ensued.

"Your bloody mad Lauren, but thank you so much."

"Okay, old man. We'll pick you up at 11.00 a.m. and head to the hotel. It should only take a few hours to get there, and then we can truly relax, by that I mean, get pissed of course."

Using a fake laugh, he answered, "Of course. I'll see you soon." They said their goodbyes and John finished drying off and getting ready. He still wasn't sure whether he was doing the right thing by going back.

They arrived at the hotel which was quite plush, John knew the area but didn't know anything about the hotel. They dumped their bags and the foursome set off towards the town centre for something to eat and a few drinks.

"Let's go in here, it looks very nice." Said Lauren excitedly.

John immediately recognised the restaurant, it was the one that John had booked for Anna and some friends, where Lilly had spoiled the party. "Yes, yes, this will do." replied John.

They all trouped in and got a table by the window.

The girls departed to get refreshed as they called it, and Matt scrutinised the menu. John looked around with memories flooding back from that night and the place hadn't changed at all. He could still hear Lilly's voice, pissed and accusing. The girls came back suitably refreshed and the night carried on. The food washed down with vino and cocktails made such a splendid night for all and also laughter prevailed.

"Right!" said Matt, "How about a swift couple in a club before we get back?" They all agreed and taxied off to SASHA, "The place to be" apparently, or so it said on the internet. They all went to the bar but the place was crammed. Matt came back to the bar with one of the waiters, clutching a few bank notes, who mysteriously found a booth for them, which they gladly settled into.

They were all pretty drunk by this point, and John departed to the toilets but as he stood at the urinals, he looked in the mirror. *"Fucking Jesus,"* he thought as he quickly turned his head. He recognised Jimmy Conran the newspaper hack going into one of the cubicle's, John swiftly moved from the urinals and headed back out into the darkness of the club then stood at the bar watching the toilet door.

Matt approached his friend, "You okay, mate?"
"Yeah, yeah, just getting some more shots for us." then out of the toilets came Mr James Conran, reporter extraordinaire, passing really close to him. John thought, *"God, I didn't think he would still be in this part of the world."*
Suddenly, Jimmy turned and faced John, "Can I get in their mate?"
"Yeah, sure, go ahead mate." replied John, relieved there was no sign of any kind of recognition at all, he moved along the bar and back to his friends. *"Phew, that was too close, but at least he didn't recognise me."*

The weekend had come to an end , John was the first to be dropped off, "That was a great weekend, thanks for a great birthday party." John pulled his bag from the boot of the car, then looked at Lauren, "It was absolutely brilliant. I'll give you all a call for a catch up and probably see you Friday. He gave a passionate kiss to Lauren and the car departed. Waving goodbye he started up his fine gravel path. He was glad to be home.

The dishevelled reporter, Jimmy Conran poked a very large lens through some bushes from a very discrete distance and the camera burst into action taking frame after frame. Talking out loud to himself, "That will do it I think." Reviewing the images in the car, "Well fuck me sideways, the sly bastard, what the fuck is he doing here?" he continued studying the images, for confirmation of his find.

John opened the front door and was greeted by a load of mail and a familiar large brown envelope. He knew only too well what that was. He threw his bag down and opened the envelope, an "Invitation to a

Celebration of Financers" the address he knew only too well. Another mission was heading his way, and he needed to go to HQ tomorrow. Meanwhile, not a million miles away, an overjoyed Jimmy Conran sped off, back to his home turf, a sinister smile on his smug face.

Chapter 14

"My name is Wandsworth, Gordon Wandsworth."
The man was in his sixties' and very well spoken.
John shook his hand, "It's nice to meet you."
"Let me just say, I have heard all about your training
and the missions you have completed, you must be
very proud."
"Yes, I'm very proud."
"My role, in this department, is to oversee the
training and manage some of the very special
missions we need to complete, and that is why you
are here today."

Sitting down next to John he continued, speaking
calmly and sincerely, starting with the mission
speech. "John, I cannot emphasise the significance of
this operation I am about to discuss. It is without
doubt, of very high importance to this country, and I
might say to the rest of the western world." John sat

up, listening intently to what the gentleman had to say.

"Our agencies have been monitoring a special man indeed." he paused a took a sharp breath and raised to his feet. "Phillip Barron." A picture appeared on a flat screen, "A man you might call a "one-man disaster zone" all because of his capabilities. Mr Barron is by no means your average villain or agent, he is quite simply, the brightest cyber and technology expert on the planet. The dangerous potential he could inflict to any state or nation is enormous, way more than any army could ever possibly produce. He could destroy civilisation as we know it, literally overnight, with some computer code, he could bring power stations to a halt, launch missiles, create phoney wars and have unstoppable control over our defences. It has been decided he must be controlled at all costs. We have no counter measures against him, and above all, we must act immediately." John didn't know what to think but more information was headed his way.

"Recent reports suggest he is been detained in Iran, where he has been imprisoned in a very high security centre, codenamed Adra, in the North West of the country. The Iranians are aware that we know of his capture, but think we have no idea of his capabilities. The arrest and imprisonment are simply cover stories. In fact, they know Barron quite well, his line of work, and what he can do. It's also understood, he has, for some reason, recently acquired Middle Eastern sympathy's and he has said, he would help them achieve any of their desired goals. This situation cannot be allowed to happen and I hope you understand and are following all of this." John nodded and sighed, just then a knock on the door. Roper along with Grenville walked in, "That's all I bloody need." thought John.

Wandsworth got up and went to greet them, "Come on in gentlemen, get yourself a coffee, we're just starting the second stage now." He walked around and looked out of the window, a clip board with notes swung in his hand.

Nervously he restarted "Okay, let's get on with this. John, are you ok?" there was silence. "Jolly good, good man. This is the brief, and what we are about to ask of you. I know it won't be a problem for your Timestop skills as I know they are exceptional. The hard part for you, and I think it would be fair to say, is that you still see yourself as a civilian. You need to mentally and morally be strong and try to understand what your involvement will mean.

"One of my tasks is to detail a process to you, of how we would like the mission to be done but obviously using your expertise to complete it. When the target is reached, you will stop time in the usual fashion, then you will then render the target useless to anyone." Wandsworth produced what looked like a pen, "This is a micro hypodermic syringe which contains a nerve agent that we have produced, especially for this mission. This drug will be administered by you alone, which in turn, will make

Phillip Barron ineffective, in simple terms it will brainwash him rendering him useless to his Iranian allies. Although he will remain alive, when you commence time, his thought process and reasoning will be wiped from his brain, he will not remember anything, not even his name, and more importantly, there will be no trace whatsoever of our intervention. The Iranians won't know what to make of it, and because he will be no use to them, unfortunately, he will then be killed. They will suspect dirty play but, and this is a big but John, it will look so inexplainable. He will be okay one minute, then the next, a rambling idiot. No suspicion of any foul play by us, and the world will move on, a little bit safer."

An eerie long silence came across the room then, John spoke up, "Why don't you just kill the poor bastard? Surely that would be better."

"Oh no, John, we can't go down that route." replied Wandsworth, "Special forces and all of that, that would certainly point towards an intrusion into their country by forces unknown. No, no, no, we couldn't have that. Why go through all of the diplomatic tosh that would undoubtedly follow, when we have secret capabilities like our brilliant Timestop people?"

John realised Wandsworth was not interested in anything he had to say or even any kind of alternative solutions. The company colours ran through him like black blood and the department was always right. Besides, all of this brief and what it contained, would have been decided days ago.

Wandsworth continued with his speech, "On a brighter note, you always wanted to meet some of your Timestop colleagues, and tomorrow you will, for they too will be going along with you on this mission, to assist with the insertion."

Grenville walked over to John which made him feel uneasy. He sat with his feet on a chair next to him. "Is everything sweet then John? You feeling good about all of this?" A prolonged silence fell between them while John thought of an answer. "I'm not a killer Grenville."

Grenville's shark like dark eyes met with John's as if it were a boxing match weigh in, staring deep into his soul. "That mission you did in Romania, all of the agents got it, I bet you didn't know that. Yes, you did the operation and it all went to plan. Unfortunately, they all got blown away, while you, Mr McAndrew, was sipping on your brandy in first class all the way home. Oh yes, and remember that poor sod of a psychiatrist lying in a pool of blood, whose head you nearly decapitated?"

Again, another awkward silence descended between them until Grenville continued with a tone of sarcasm, "Oh no, no, of course you're not a fucking killer." John had completely forgot about the psychiatrist. Grenville saw the recognition on his face, "Don't try the angel game with me. Timestopper or not, this is what it's all about, remember, the security of our country at any cost." John bowed his head, "Bastards!"
Grenville got closer, "Are you saying you don't want this mission John? Just say, we could always get

someone else if you prefer." scratching his chin, he continued, "which I suppose, would make you redundant to us and that would fucking suit me just fine. Bye, bye, Timestopper shit." menacingly sliding his finger along his neck.

"Okay, Grenville. That's enough, I think he's got the message." responded Roper as he watched Grenville getting a little carried away with John. Grenville pushed the chair over to the other side of the room and sat down.

"Right gentlemen, if we could just stick to the briefing." nervously Wandsworth continued. "Right John," pausing he glanced around the room at Roper and Grenville the air was thick.

"Okay, the next part is getting you there, and inside the security centre. The only issue on the mission is the Timestop footprint you have, would have no effect on the guards on the other side of the centre, this is where our three other stoppers will be tasked. They are not up to the same skill as you John, and they can only Timestop for about ten minutes or so.

They can stop time with the guards, allowing you enough time to get into position."

Wandsworth was starting to look very concerned, he continued hesitantly, "I must tell you, if they can't hold time off long enough, which is probable, and time restarts they will most definitely be killed by the guards. Their position would be compromised and it will most likely look like a failed capture attempt. They don't know this, but the documents they will be carrying with them will verify a paramilitary force. The group have no idea of what the possible consequences are for them." another long silence, "Quite simply John, they are cannon fodder to get the job done." He was feeling uneasy about all of this and it didn't sit well with him.

"Surely you have better Timestoppers who can fulfil the task and hold off longer?"
"Oh yes, yes, we have John. They, like you, are all unique but wouldn't be used, unfortunately you will never work with them or meet them. The whole

Timestop phenomenon is exclusive and certainly a secret asset to any country. Unfortunately, the Timestoppers that have the poorest ability, also have a limited life. We would never put an experienced Timestopper in jeopardy, they are just too valuable, and need to be protected. Do you understand?"

John knew he had no choice but to agree with everything in the brief, his heart went out to the poor saps he had been desperate to meet for all these years, and now, he knew he would never meet the ones he needed to talk to.

Roper and Grenville approached, Roper sympathetically said you'll be fine it's just part of the job. It's what you were chosen for, bending over. Grenville once again ran his finger over his throat it's a shit life get on with it, and don't fuck it up. John didn't rise to the baiting, and just replied, "no problem, thanks a lot". The meeting adjourned, Wandsworth disappeared into the distance with his buddies. John cursing under his breath returned to his humble abode.... not happy at all.

The phone rang several times before the reply, "DC Myers speaking."

"Listen Tom, I've got photos of him, that John McAndrew, remember him?"

"Is this the guy who got done for embezzlement and went to the states?" said DC Myers.

"Yeah, that's him."

"Are you fucking stupid, oh yes, I forgot, of course you are? Listen shitface, ask yourself this. Why would he risk coming back to this country, only to get arrested and locked up forever?

Nah, Jimmy, you've got it wrong mate, it's just someone who looks like him."

"No, no, no, Tom, it was him. I tell you what, meet up with me and I will show you the pictures. It's him, I'm positive and I have the pictures to prove it."

"Okay, Jimbo, but if you're wasting my time with

this, I'll kick you in the nuts, understand? I'll see you later pea brain."

Jimmy was scrutinizing the dozen or so images when DC Tom Myers walked in and the pub descended into the usual silence. "Why does that always happen when you walk in Tom?"

Myers looked around at the many faces glancing at him, "It's them fuckers. They know when the old bill's in town and Tom Myers, bastard extraordinaire has arrived." Laughing, he grabbed his usual free pint. "Okay, let's see what you've got."

Jimmy quickly passed the photos to him, "Hmm, hmm." DC Myers studied the photos that was in front of him, "Yeah, I suppose it could be him, but I am not certain."

"How could we find out then?"

"What about his ex-bird, what was her name again, Winny or Trinny or something?"

"It was Lilly."

"Yeah, well go and check with her then."

"Nah, that would be a bad bet now Tom. She's in

with a right crowd of hard cases."

"And when has hard cases ever bothered me James, no fucker gets the better of Tom Myers."

"But, it's the Malone's from the East End."

Tom thought for a second, "Maybe your right. You know where McAndrew lives?"

"Yeah, it's beautiful house. So, I guess crime does pay." joked Jimmy.

"Right here's the plan, get yourself up to his place and see if he reacts when he clocks you. Believe me, you will know if it's him by his reaction. If your certain it's him, tell him we need to meet to discuss some unfinished business, okay? After all, he can't deny anything now, it was all over the papers when the serious crime squad got involved, but they never got him, so the reward money is coming our way, Jimmy boy."

John was quietly sitting in his rear garden when he heard the front doorbell but he knew he wasn't expecting anyone, so sat it out. His garden gate opened to reveal a person he had hoped he would never ever see again, Jimmy Conran. He jumped up and went across,

"Who the fuck are you? Don't you know your trespassing?"

"Why don't you call the Police then, John."

"Do I know you?"

"You know me very well Mr McAndrew, so come off it."

"I'm afraid your wrong, I've never seen you before in my life."

Jimmy held up his mobile phone in the air, "Should I call the police for you John?"

John turned with his back to him and was deep in thought, *"Where the fuck was Grenville when you really needed him?"* but he knew, he had no options, because this little shit didn't bluff, he would call the police and then we would be stuck, compromised and the termination order came to mind. He turned and faced the reporter. "Okay, what do you want?"

"Quite simply, Mr McAndrew, money. I don't need explanations or stories. Money is our only interest?" John sat back down, "Jimmy, for once in your life, I want you to listen, and listen very carefully. Things have changed now, and I work for a system that you or anyone else can't blackmail. I can't tell you anything about my work, but these are professional people who could make life very difficult for you, even kill you, and any accomplices you may have, they are above the law. So, I would suggest you forget all about what you know, or think you know and disappear very quickly, and nothing more will be said."

A long pause followed and Jimmy, with cigarette in mouth, clapped his hands very slowly, "Is that it? Is that the best you can do?" Jimmy began laughing in John's face.

"Now then John, I don't think you're able to tell me what to do, I hold all the cards. I have the proof, and the bloody serious crime squad is on my side, so this is what's going to happen. Because you've been away for so long, our original offer has increased slightly, just to cover expenses and any interest, you understand. One million pounds sounds about right, in cash, okay? A nice round number. I'll be in touch; you've got one week." Jimmy exited through the garden gate

John knew what he had to do, so he rang Roper and explained the problem, with the emphasises of placing the blame right in the departments court. Roper was on his way and John was beginning to panic and he just hoped, he could get away with it.

On arrival Roper seemed unconcerned, certainly not what John expected. "Okay, John lets sort this lot out once a for all. It would appear we didn't sweep up after your identification changed, sometimes this happens, but don't worry about it. Right, give me all the details, names, localities and everything you know about this scally and his mates." A few hours later, Roper took his paperwork and departed, saying to John on the way out, "You concentrate on your upcoming event and we will sort this little lot out."

===

The old mare was jumping as usual, after the usual brief silence for the entrance of DC Myers. After sitting and taking a sip from his usual free pint. He listened intently to what Jimmy had to say. He replied, with shock and disbelief, "One million..." DC Myers rubbed his hands over his face then continued, "And McAndrew went for it? Tell you what Jimmy, I've underestimated you. What you gonna do with your hundred grand?"

"Hundred grand!!" Jimmy repeated.

"I'm only kidding ya old scrote, we'll go be going fifty-fifty, obviously." Tom Myers had other ideas. He had no intentions on giving this idiot five hundred grand.

"Tell you what, McAndrew looked scared, it wasn't like the last time. He said, he was in a different crowd now and they were dangerous."

"Who the fuck is worried about that James?"

pointing at himself, "Hello, Her Majesty's Constabulary, sitting right here." They both raised their glasses and began laughing.

Roper was hard at work at his desk when Grenville came in, "You wanted to see me?"

"Yes, yes. It looks like we've got a situation developing with McAndrew, and his previous identity."

Grenville reacted quickly, "Do you want him done?"

"No, no, nothing like that, it's not his fault. The department didn't clear all his past business, and it is ghosting him." He went through the whole file with Grenville. "Can you deal with it?" Grenville nodded, "I'll get a squad on it."

"I want all possible targets removed. No more problems okay?"

"No problem, they're gone."

Roper telephoned John to let him know that he

shouldn't be getting bothered again with any threats, but reminded him, if there was anything, anything at all, any little secrets, the department needed to know about it, and it would be in his best interests to say now. "If something goes wrong again John, the next contract Grenville will have, will be yours, do you understand?"

"Yes, I understand." said John, "There's nothing else."

Chapter 15

Tactical trial runs had finished for "Operation Darkness" and John had to meet the Timestopper trio at an operational base in the South of England. From there, they would be transported to Southern Turkey by aircraft. They would be met by a local military unit, who will get them to the border of Iran. From there, they would be accompanied, undercover, by friendly forces to the security base. John was absolutely shitting himself; this was like nothing he had done before; not even Romania came anywhere close.

They met in a ops room for introductions. As John entered, there were two women and a man who introduced themselves as the security group. They only knew John as Operative 01, presumably for security reasons. He shook their hands with pleasantries and small talk and as expected, they all knew their role, but John cast an eye across them, they all looked like rabbits in the headlights He was already nervous, but nothing like them. It didn't help that John knew their fate and this would be their last hours together, this was shit. With no time to think about it, a squaddie rounded them all up, and they were off to Southern Turkey.

On arrival, it was nightfall, they were split into two groups. John set off with a guard of four into the Turkish darkness and the security group were placed on a truck and driven off in a different direction. Radios were buzzing with chatter, all in Turkish, but as they approached the handover point everything hushed. The guard signalled for John to keep quiet, while the others exited from the vehicle and cut through a wire fence. His main guard had told him to clamber through the netting and someone would meet him on the other side. He informed John; the others were already in place.

John followed the orders and went through the fence

and the unlit vehicle turned, drove down the road slightly then waited. By now, he was extremely nervous and then a soldier, who was heavily camouflaged with green beret approached,

"You okay mate? I'm your contact."

"Yes, what now?" John asked apprehensively.

"Follow me. Listen, just stay cool and you'll be okay." They walked up a small hill.

"Get down on the ground mate." John complied, no questions asked, "Right, follow me, just crawl up to the top." John followed his mentor and reached the brow of the hill.

Speaking quietly, he pointed downwards, "That's where you'll be going mate." he continued to point to a large, well-lit and fenced in compound. "Let's hope your friends can do their bit." He said smiling, "I'm sure they can." Just then there was some chatter on the radio and the guy said, "Okay, it's showtime, you're on. Apparently, they've done their bit so chop, chop. You're on your own now."

John headed down to the compound as rehearsed and

walked into a Timestop zone, he could feel it and he knew they had managed to stop time. *"Great, the guards are motionless."* He quickly located the block where the target was known to be and calmly walked in, making sure his Timestop was in place, he marked his watch. The place stunk like shit and obviously Barron wasn't fussy about his conditions. He located the room, and there in front of him, sat a young man, exactly the same as the ID photos he had received. He looked at his watch and five minutes had passed. He immediately removed the nerve agent also the applicator from his belt and now he was holding it, looking at it, looking at Barron.

John hesitated and the sweat was dripping from his brow, his heart was racing as he grasped the syringe, putting it millimetres from Barron's skin. He thought to himself, "What am I doing? Oh god, please forgive me." and stuck the needle into Barron's vein. No obvious movement, as expected as John withdrew the deadly apparatus and placed it safely back into its holder.

Suddenly in the background a thunderous amount of automatic weapon fire was breaking the silence of night, "Oh god." His objective complete and time stopped, all that was left was for John to make a hasty retreat from this abysmal place, knowing three people had probably just lost their lives and one person when he awakes would be wishing he would lose his. He scrambled back to the RV point, started time and met up with his contact. "Fucking hell, are you okay mate?" asked the solider.

John was drained white, "Come on, let's get you out of here, they withdrew from the area, gunfire all around the complex, shouting and cheers prevailed. John was ushered to a waiting vehicle and headed for the base.

On arrival, he was shocked to find one of his Timestopper colleagues, had made it back, one of the girls. She was being quickly ushered down the corridor with guards at her side. The military contact told him, she knew they couldn't hold time off any longer, but before it started again, she managed to grab a weapon. On the regain of time, there was surprise at first and the guards realised they had intruders in their mist, and got several rounds into her companions before she opened fire with her weapon whilst running for her life. John remained shook up, the mental picture of young Mr. Barron, and all of tonight's events, time to go for the plane.

Standing at the foot of the aircraft, John was asking the soldiers about the girl. "Where is she? You need to wait for her." But the girl was nowhere to be seen, which seemed odd. The soldiers didn't have any information of her whereabouts, or their missing passenger, and speedily packed John on to the aircraft. John thought she must be returning by a different way. The plane lifted, and the ground swiftly disappeared, He thanked god they were on their way back. Meanwhile, in a forest near to the security centre, the lifeless gunshot body of a brave young girl was un-ceremoniously being dumped in the thick woodland undergrowth.

John wondered if his mission had succeeded. He knew he had administered the nerve agent as per instruction. When time restarted, he was well away from the scene. How was Barron now? Had it worked? And did it solve the problem it was designed to do? but above all, where was that brave girl?

It had been a while and John still hadn't had any debrief or news from the department. He also didn't know what was happening with Jimmy Conran, which unnerved him. He had been with his friends and Lauren quite a lot, over the previous weeks. It was getting really serious with her now, and he believed she wanted their relationship to go further, but John knew too well, living together and the basic things that couples do, was a big negative in his world, his employers wouldn't allow it. It was okay for them to say get on with your life, but John knew he couldn't. This is as far as he could go with any sort of closeness, yet he desperately wanted to move on. Another weekend passed with the situation the same and then finally a text came from the department to debrief at the centre.

He arrived promptly and was asked to go to Mr Wandsworth's office. Gordon Wandsworth sat behind his huge desk. His files in his trays overflowing, most of them had top secret headings.

"Hello John, how are you today?"

John immediately replied, "A bit pissed off to be honest. Since my return I haven't heard a thing from here about how the mission went, was it successful? and the blackmail attempt's?"

"Okay John, I think I have all the answers to your questions, now that we have had intel. Firstly, your mission was an absolute success, the poor Mr Barron did survive, well for a couple of days at least. The plan worked perfectly, and a first class result from yourself, but the Iranians, as expected, couldn't suffer all the poor info from him, couldn't understand what had happened, so it was bye, bye, for Mr Barron."

Eagerly John said, "What about the girl survivor, how's she?"

Wandsworth looked away and confirmed, "She's dead John. She had to be eliminated on site. We couldn't let them think someone got away, so alas she died for the cause."

John stood up, his anger venting, "Bollocks!" said John, "You're all a pack of bastards. She'd done more than her bit and managed to escape, your cruel shits."

Wandsworth mood changed as he turned to John. Raising his voice to a level John had never heard before, he replied, "Your alive, aren't you? The worlds a safer place, and that's all that matters. McAndrew you've got to realise it's just the way it is, not only in this country, it simply has to be done, things like this are done all over the world regularly and it will never be found out in the public domain, well, only if it ever goes wrong." John was taken aback at Wandsworth's abruptness; he had always been so calm.

Changing tone once again to his serious voice Wandsworth announced, "The other issue has proved more of a problem John, by the time our staff got some intel on Mr Conran, he and his accomplice have gone into hiding, they must have known they were a target, and have went to ground. Your friend Conran did call the police, who were interested in their comments, but our internal officers sorted that issue for now. We need to find these two jokers, as a matter of urgency."

Two miserable blokes sat in a car park eating fish and chips, wind hurling around them, "God, it looks cold out there."

"Jesus Christ Jimmy, we're supposed to be millionaires now, what the fuck went wrong?"

"I know Tom, but there's been lots of people asking around town, checking up on not just me, but both of us."

"I know…" retorted Myers, "…you stupid shit, I am

a copper you know! They've already asked the plod at the station and they told them I was off work sick."

Jimmy's worried tones continued, "Listen Tom, somebody wants us desperately, and I think its McAndrew's lot." said the worried Jimmy.

"Shut your face, what lot is this then?"

"Remember, he said he now worked for a system. What the fucks a system Tom? Is it the mafia, drug gangs or something else? Anyway, I think he was telling the truth, and some hard heads are heading for both of us." Jimmy was scaring himself to death.

"Calm down Jimbo." He waited for complete silence, and then he addressed Jimmy. "Listen, I've been thinking, how's this for a plan, how's about we fuck off on a nice little holiday for a few weeks, to France. My mate's got a small villa there, that he hardly uses and I'm sure he would let us have it for a few weeks. The heat will die down and that lot will have bigger fish to fry than us. We'll be all forgotten about there, how does that sound?"

Jimmy perked up a bit, "Yeah, yeah, that sounds

good, we could stay for a while, but how will we get their Tom? I mean, without anyone knowing?" Myers began laughing then said, "I don't think Mr McAndrew's lot would have mates on border control, we'll just take the ferry, no one would ever know we were gone."

"Just one thing Tom, if we do manage to get over there, will that mean we'll forget about the blackmail deal with McAndrew?" Seconds later, Jimmy was feeling his throbbing testicles which had been attacked by a very pissed off policeman, "Fucking numb nut"

John went up his path to his only sanctuary away from government departments, chancers and everyday life. Settling into a nice glass of wine, his mind began to wander. Wondering, where all of this will end, would he end up dead too? He had done his job, but leaving a trail of destruction behind, talented people dead, brave young girls killed for no reason. The world was indeed safe, but how long before another nutcase or specialist comes to ruin it.

He was thinking dangerously, to go it alone, to get normal, was it out of the question? Could he escape all this madness and come out of the other end? He thought of the people he had met on his journey, and where they will be in the future, if in fact they are still alive. John needed re-assurances and thoughts drifted towards his first ever contact Catina. *"I wonder if she's still part of a grand scheme somewhere, working for her cause."* He remembered Grenville saying they had all been killed. *"I wonder…"* John remembered that night in the hotel with her, and the note.

Going to his wardrobe, he found the suit that he had worn, and there in the inside pocket was the note, and the phone number. John picked up the phone, was about to dial, but hesitated. He had been with the department long enough to know it would be foolish to think his phone wasn't tapped, they trusted no one, he just wondered if normal life can go on, in this mysterious, murderous world. *"I'll ring another day."*

He went to bed, alone with his thoughts, so much so, his head hurt. It was like Timestopper old days, but now, he knew exactly what his talents were for, and who would be using them, who was benefiting from them, and who was merely a pawn in a world size game of chess.

He woke the next morning, refreshed, but remained perplexed and worried of his future. After breakfast, he took a long walk around the lovely countryside near his home, in the hope it would clarify what to do next. He knew he couldn't go back to normality, he would be hounded and probably terminated. God, he hated that word. He arrived at the old river crossing and looking into the water, he visualized the many images of his life to date, the gift, as he used to refer to it, had practically destroyed him, although he had everything he could want. The gift had allowed him to commit murder, ruin lives, destroy relationships and finish what the old John McAndrew was about. He knew what he did wasn't for him, but at least the world could breathe easy in their beds, in the knowledge that crazy people, the hurtful, the unpleasant situations, had all been taken care of. He concluded, that if this was to be his life, at the very least, he certainly needed a break from it. He needed to get away, all alone, and get off this dreadful dark roundabout for a while, he hoped it would help him.

Chapter 16

One look back on the steps, as he boarded his first-class flight to Naples, ready to get some well-earned relaxation and recuperation. His lovely girlfriend Lauren, was aware he'd gone away, but she thought it was for work, special finance, deals, etcetera, but if she only knew the truth. Sitting in his luxurious surroundings he felt a bit of a renegade knowing he hadn't told the department, his bosses and keepers, and these thoughts pleased him. It would have took the edge off it had he asked for permission take a holiday and they would have loved that, he thought to himself, as the aircraft began to raise into the sky, *"Fuck them all."*

Four hours later, he had arrived at his hotel suite which would be his home for two weeks. He settled into the very expensive room, had a few drinks, before crashing out on the comfortable bed totally exhausted.

Over the next few days, John found the peace and tranquillity he sought, just doing what normal people do. He filled some of his time sightseeing, walking around the lovely city and just chilling with the rest of the many tourists. He had a couple of calls from Lauren, just general chatter, asking if he was okay and the other usual stuff, but he also had countless missed calls from the department but strangely enough, no text, which he found odd as they always sent texts.

"Mr McAndrew." the receptionist called as he walked into the lobby, "Excuse me sir, could I leave this message with you?" she handed John an envelope, with Mr J McAndrew and his room number on it, John politely said thank you and headed off to his suite. The letter contained an invitation to a drink's reception in the cocktail lounge for the hotels special guests and a small note

saying, "Please come, signed by the manager Mr
Ratzini.

"Ah, Mr McAndrew, so nice to meet you, allow me
to introduce you to some very special guests we have
staying with us now." The pleasantries continued
with other special guests. "Mr. McAndrew, may I
introduce you to Dr Victor Petrov, "Hello, I'm
pleased to meet you Mr McAndrew." Shaking his
hand, John thought Victor stood out from the crowd,
he had quite an edge about him, quite aloof, a lot
older than John, he seemed very experienced and
confident. He asked John if he would like to come
through to the private lounge for some proper drinks
while the other special guests continued to chat away
and boast to each other about the size of their bank
balances. Intrigued by the man, John agreed and
decided to follow him into the cocktail lounge.

Victor asked him about what he did for a living,
general chit chat, and then, out of the blue said
something very bizarre …he said that he sensed they

both had something in common, something very special. John looked puzzled,

"I don't understand, that's a strange thing to say, what do you mean? I am a finance salesman from the UK, I wouldn't have a clue of your occupation or even where you're from?"

An immediate response came back," I am Russian. I am a Doctor of Science."

"Okay…" John replied, still perplexed, "…but how on earth could we have something in common, except for staying in the same hotel?"

Victor glanced around the mostly empty room and then said, "John, I will not insult your intelligence. I was one of the first Timestoppers in the world, many years ago, and worked for the Russians, then the American government, displaying my skills, and like you, I realised what I did was unique, but in the end, it was no good."

John raised an eyebrow and he thought to himself while looking at this man, *"After all these years of wanting to meet another Timestopper, and its happened on my holidays.* " The Russian interrupted his thoughts, "If we were not using our talents to help them, I can guarantee, they would find some other method of accomplishing their goal. Be it yourself or your government, I can tell you now, your days are numbered, this work is very dangerous, and I should know."

John couldn't believe what he was hearing, he had to be genuine, he knew too much, Not denying or confirming his story John said, "I'm all ears Mr Petrov."

"No, no, please call me Victor." He started to explain his Timestop experiences, which were the same as Johns early years. He explained the Russian government had discovered him early in life, when he was just fifteen years old. In the name of the Russian state, he was taken from his family, and on reaching his twentieth birthday, he was on the brink of time stopping for almost two hours, but they still weren't satisfied. He was coached and plied with substances to achieve their ultimate objective, to go back in time, to reverse time, to wind the clock back, instead of just stopping it, and they did it.

"John, they got me to recoil time back almost one hour, and I really don't know how, it was a mystery, just like the first time stopping days, but they did it and as you can imagine, once it had been done, I was theirs, like a toy to play with. You become desensitised, and meaningless, that is why I defected to the USA, but in my naivety, I didn't realise the stakes would be the same, only in a different language." Both Victor and John took a long stiff gulp of drink before Victor continued.

"After ten or so years with them, I decided to make it my business to escape this unimportant game and made my way to Europe to try and blend in with normal people, but I had to be always one step ahead. On occasion, turning back time to escape their capture traps, constantly in hiding, but believe me John, it was better than working for them and even today, they still hunt me."

John was now sold on his story, "But how did you

know about me?"

"I have followed your career very closely John McAndrew, I have been aware of all your operations throughout the world. I have been unseen, and un-noticed by the authorities on every mission, every target. How it was done, and knowing how it had affected you, knowing you will get no post assignment help from them, which I think you have realised now. You are a machine to them and if you break, or hiccup, you'll be scrapped."

"But why follow me to this holiday hotel?"

"That's simple. I needed to warn you of the dangerous paths and how your life will pan out if your course is not changed. I didn't have anyone to assist me in my life, but I can help you if you will allow me. You're doing exactly as I did, trying to get away from it and running away from the torments in your head, but whatever you do is only temporary, and you know it. You need a fresh start, you need to escape your captors John, let them go."

"That's easy for you to say." John replied, "How the hell could I do that? Escape from the Government?"

"John, I can guide you, I have people who can help, just for this purpose."

"Right, you're really spooking me out now. Is this even for real and how do I know your genuine? You could be the opposition trying to get rid of me."

"John, you must know by now, if any government wanted you out of the way, you would have been gone by now. Why would I make myself known to you, break my cover, and potentially put us both at risk if I wasn't sincere. If you would like to take this conversation further could we meet say, in a couple of days. It'll give you time to think about what we have discussed tonight."

John thought for a while, "No harm in talking, Dr Petrov is there? I'll be here."

Tom Myers headed up the winding pathway to a very charming villa, followed closely by Jimmy Conran dragging two large suitcases, cigarette in mouth, trying to talk at the same time, "This looks just what we're after Tom."

A drunken Tom Myers fumbled around in his pocket for the front door key, eventually poking it into the hole and turning the lock, the door flew open, "Oh fucking Jesus, Jimmy, put that fucking fag out!"

"This is the nine o' clock news" "Two men were tragically killed today, believed to be from the UK on holiday. It appears a potentially serious gas leak went unnoticed for days, only to be ignited by a discarded cigarette. According to the local fire officer in St. Cezaire, in Cote d'Azur, France. The fire took over two hours to control and has been left with extensive damage, this property is so badly damaged the only course would be demolition. The inquest on the two men will begin next week, with accidental death being probable cause."

Walking around the port of Naples, John was trying to understand Victor, he was undoubtedly real and honest, he didn't think he would be a threat and in his own way, maybe he was trying to help. Anyway, he was meeting him tonight, but in a local quiet restaurant. Hopefully getting an insight how to navigate forward. Johns phone burst into action a text from the department. *It would seem our secondary problem has been successfully eliminated. All threats have been isolated... Hope Naples is nice and hot.* How the fuck? is there anything they don't know? he wondered, that's one question for Victor I'd like an answer too.

John was hanging around the lobby of the hotel, when a familiar Russian voice said,
"Good evening, Mr McAndrew, I have taken the liberty of booking a taxi, I hope that's okay." "Yes, fine." John said, "that looks like ours pulling up now." They both climbed in, and the Russian said the name of the restaurant, which the taxi driver knew well. They went off in the Naples evening and headed for one of the best restaurants in Naples.

Once they arrived at their destination and seated at their table, Victor began his pitch. "Have you thought about what I was saying John?"

"I have…" John replied, "…and I have quite a few questions you may or may not answer."

The Russian opened his briefcase and pulled out a file marked top secret. Staring at the doctor, John said, "Do you think that is wise? in the middle of a restaurant, Victor?"

He smiled at John and said, "It's not all smoke and mirrors John, nobody even has a clue what where doing or talking about, so stop panicking my friend." He rifled through some more papers, and then John thought to himself, *"Maybe I should play my trump card."* with that, he stopped time. As usual everything was still, including Victor. John grasped the briefcase and started looking through the secret papers, he was stunned when Victor suddenly said, "Ah ha, my plan worked." John looked around; time remained stopped except for Victor. "I knew you would do something like this, just as a test."

John immediately started time and apologised to Victor. "I am so sorry I had to do that, surely you know why."

The Russian let out one loud belly laugh and said, "The jokes on you McAndrew, for all those secret papers are all fake. Do you really think I'm crazy as well?"

With that the two of them just laughed and somehow felt at ease with each other, knowing there would be no further tricks.

Following their meal, John got to business. "So, then Victor, how does the department know where I am?"

"They know where you are twenty-four hours a day John, through technology, global mapping or tracking you might call it. Your phone, your suitcase, free access to border control information, it's the government, they know your every move, but it does have its sinister side, and this is the sad bit. Following mine and many other defections, the worlds agencies decided to have ultimate control over there so-called operatives, time stopping or not.

Ten years ago, they started to fit ETD's or electronic termination devices into an operative's body, unawares to the person. If someone didn't comply, considered defecting, spying or telling the world, a code is all that would be needed. A signal would be sent, just like a happy birthday message on a mobile and an electronic capsule inside the body would release a nerve agent into the blood stream, rendering the operative dead, and I mean, well and truly. It would leave no trace whatsoever. I have no doubt you will have one of these devices fitted, although disturbing, and un-nerving, I know you are quite safe at this time, so our number one priority task would be to remove this piece of shit."

John was silenced with shock and wished he had never come on holiday or met Dr Petrov. He had no choice but to believe him and it didn't surprise him that the department would do such a thing, after all, they were known to be ruthless.

Searching for answers, "When did they do this to

me? When did they insert this deadly device? Surely, I would have known."

Victor responded, "Do you know Roper?"

"Yes, yes, I know him."

"Did you know he could Timestop as well?"

Johns eyebrow raised, "I had a vague idea from when I was first recruited."

"Well, he would be your man. You weren't skilled enough to know you were in a time stop zone, like before with us. He would have done the deed, well at least stopped time and a Doctor Lanmore, I think he's called, again another Timestopper would have administered the tiny capsule into your veins as you know with Timestop, no blood, and little chance of it going wrong."

"Is there any chance of it going off accidentally?" John said worryingly holding his arm,

"Oh no, not a hope in hell, it could sit there forever, until you died naturally, so don't fret about that, they wouldn't let that happen."

"Victor, you've convinced me, where do we go from here? the sooner the better."

"Look John, try not to worry too much, after all, you didn't know anything until tonight, and at least, I can sort it. Enjoy our drink, I will make the relevant arrangements and be in touch in a weeks' time. Let's just have a good night, okay?"

Chapter 17

John arrived back home and was met at the airport by Lauren. She looked good, in fact stunning.

"Before we go back, do you fancy a drink in town?"

"Bloody right, I do." said John, "Naples is a lovely place, but the drink is rubbish." They sped off in a taxi to a dazzling bar on the edge of town, had a few drinks and caught up with all the gossip and news.

John stared at her; "Would you like to stay over in a hotel before we go home?"

Smiling, she said, "I thought you were never going to ask."

The bedroom door closed, and a passionate door flung open. John felt something, it was a sense of normality and love, how pleasant it was to be normal for once.

A text message from Roper reminded him where he was suppose be this morning, he felt different today, calmly walking into a briefing room. Roper looked up, "We've been trying to contact you McAndrew." said Roper, moving papers around his desk. "I'm led to believe you've been on holiday."

"Yeah, that's right." John quickly said, "I took a couple of weeks off as my mission appointments were zero for this month."

Roper turned to him, "This is not a fucking nine to five job McAndrew. We could have had something urgent, something very important we wanted you to complete."

"So, do you want me to sit in the house all day, pretending to do finance deals and never go out?"

Roper rose from his seat, his military voice appeared, "Don't get fucking smart with me arsehole, remember who you're talking to. I will decide when you go for a break, this department rules, okay, you fucking got that?"

John nodded and started to walk away, "Where the fuck do you think you're going? sit the fuck down." In machine like movements he sat down, which he could tell was pissing Roper off, "Right, you clever shit, here is your next mission." he slung across the table a folder. "Albeit small, it is well within your capabilities. Now study, digest, and get out of my fucking sight."

John casually walked over, picked up the folder, then walked out the door. Climbing into his car he checked the required mission statement, no details as they would follow, all in this country. Mockingly he said to himself, "Christ, I've hit the jackpot with this one."

He headed back to his home and studied the missions, his mind was distracted and firmly fixed on Lauren.

It had been two weeks since his meeting with Victor and he was beginning to think it may have been some sort of test to see how mentally strong he was. Going off Ropers reaction to John today, the current situation was not good.

The doorbell rang, it was the postman with his usual delivery of letters, one brown envelope, as expected, and the rest just finance blurb. The obvious brown one contained all the intel and info for the up-coming mission which he threw on the table. Sorting through the rest, he found an unexpected mail from a company called "KNOW YOUR PAST". John was quite suspicious and opened it, inside there was a letter from Dr Victor Petrov:

Hello John

Hope you are well, sorry it's been longer than expected for this letter, but I have been making the many arrangements as discussed on your behalf. Firstly, and more importantly, you will need to come to Geneva, Switzerland, and meet up with me. We can then go ahead with the first part of your refurbishment. We need to remove the internal problem, which will make you safe from any external influences, this is painless and should only take one afternoon of your time.

We can then talk about phase two, which would see a relocation in a remote country, away from all this unpleasantness. I can at this early stage, offer an additional place for anyone you would like to take with you, and of course, would be expected to be trusted. Once again, your identity would be altered, with no reference to any previous lives.

I would suggest you prepare for the transfer of any monies, banked, or owing to the account at the bottom of the page and access to this will only be possible by yourself. Further funding to you would come from myself employing you as a freelance Timestopper for corporate clients, hopefully in the future. Sorry to have to communicate all of this by letter, but I know you'll understand the security aspect of it all. Please find below all the details you will need,

Yours Sincerely
Victor

John put Victors letter in a safe place and began to scrutinize the files for his mission. It was top secret, the highest level. Target: A top government finance officer in the North of England. They wanted files removed from his computer system and then held on a memory drive for further investigation. Probable cause, funding terrorism,

"At least I don't have to do anything terrible" John thought. They wanted the target and his department to carry on as normal. Totally unexpected, but they needed information that he was channelling government funds to an extremist organisation, and they needed to know all about it, especially, who was involved.

The police were not to find out about any of this, well not yet. The job had to be done in two days' time and the only foreseeable problem was, the mission date collided with Victors meeting in Geneva. John wondered if he could possibly do both, maybe with a private flight or something, he would have to work on this one, and sharpish.

He checked all the major airlines for flights to Geneva and as luck would have it, he found a flight out from the nearest airport to the mission. He knew he was unable to contact Victor, so he couldn't change anything, he would call Victor from a public phone, later tonight, *"Great, that's that all sorted."* His next job was much more important, a phone call to Lauren, he was hooked, and he was hoping round two was on the cards for tonight.

She opened the door and a passionate kiss ensued, "Come on in, John, I've got some wine chilling. Are you okay?" Their embraces began, and footsteps went up to the bedroom, the door firmly shut, as was John's mind, and the special call to Victor.

Meanwhile, the department mobile in his house, was bursting with noise, text after text came rushing into his inbox, all concerning the upcoming mission, but the phone was all alone, unlike John, the phone was the last thing on his mind.

He returned to the house next morning and found his department phone on the floor, it had rung so many times it had fell off the dresser. Eighteen text messages, he read them all. The mission had changed, it was today and he should have been there now, "Oh fuck, shit, shit, shit."

He called Roper, after a while, the familiar voice, "Don't fucking tell me, you bastard, you're not there are you? You're getting close to me not liking you John, and that could be very dangerous. Get yourself there now, get it done, and come straight to me when you get back." he hung up.

John stopped his car just outside the village and phoned Victor, who answered quite promptly. "Hi, its John."

"Oh, you are in the shit, aren't you?" said Victor.

"What? How the fuck do you know that?"

"I know what they know John. Don't worry, I've put our meeting back twenty-four hours to give you a chance, just do what you must, and get over her as soon as you can."

"Sorry Victor, I was going to ring last night, but I got tied up with something."

"Yes, yes, yes, of course SHE did." Laughing he hung up.

"How the fuck does he know these things?" John said out loud looking at the phone.

Continuing on he drove up the motorway as quickly as allowed and arrived at the office block. He approached the main doors; it was bustling and very busy. He knew exactly where the target office was. He went up to the sixth floor, the lift doors opened, he stepped out of the lift and went over to the water fountain. He immediately stopped time, no sound, no one moving, he swiftly went to the target.

Private office, was on the door, and behind it sat an executive, totally still. John wheeled him away, to get to the computer. Going into the file system he downloaded everything on to the portable drive he had been supplied with. The computer informed him politely that it would be five minutes to download all of the requested files. John sat on the edge of the desk, being careful not to disturb anything around it, "Hurry up, you bastard slow computer."

A few moments later and, a ping from the computer signalled the download was complete, so he took the drive, put the target back in his position, knowing in a few weeks' time, this poor sods life will be changing for the worse, which was a good thing, he was an unscrupulous man. John got his stuff together and walked out of the building, casually starting time as he passed the water fountain. His task was complete, now for the hard part, Roper!

John knocked on the door, like a naughty schoolboy waiting to meet the head. "Come in." the dullest tones of Roper and oh no, Grenville was there too, smirking as if he already knew what was about to happen, Roper spoke up,

"Right, McAndrew, you've been warned on a few occasions, and let me tell you, if you were military personnel, I would be letting Grenville here pull your balls off and feed them to the security dogs. Do you get my drift?" John was about to speak and was Grenville spoke, "Shut. The. Fuck. UP."

Roper continued, "McAndrew, if you have a problem doing this specialised work, speak up, and we will consider our options but I have to say, you and your kind are needed in this operation." and his tone raised, "But, this department will not be jerked off, do you understand? You are aware of what we can do, remember you ARE expendable, got it? This is your last warning, next time, it will be him you'll deal with." pointing at Grenville. "Now give me the drive, fuck off home, and have a think about what your future is within this department."

John made a quick getaway muttering to himself down the corridor, *"I know what my next move is mister, no more thinking about it, it's all over."* Driving straight to the airport, stayover bag in hand he boarded the Geneva flight and hopefully freedom.

When he arrived in Geneva, he called Victor, "Just stay put John, and I will send a car over for you, and then we can talk." The car arrived and sped through the night to a magnificent mountain hotel which Victor had based himself in. Meeting John in the lobby, Victors friendly tones were a joy to John's ears,

"Come on in my friend. I believe they have been given you a bit of a hard time, anyway you're here now, and that is good. Tonight, you will stay, and tomorrow we get the scans done, then, we can remove this terrible thing from your body. It will be painless, and all done by microsurgery, just a small incision will do the job and then, dear friend, you will be out of their control."

John was shown to his room where once unpacked, he met with Dr Petrov for drinks. "I still don't understand your motivation with all this Victor. I know you must have experienced many bad times in your day, but why bother? You could save yourself a great deal of hassle."

John, my friend, I do very well with my current Timestop deals, with many international clients, and respectable businesses. It keeps me financially healthy, and this in turn helps to keep my many dangers at arm's length.

"I know." Responded John.

"When you discovered your gift, you would have automatically thought it must be limited across the world, but it's not John. Many governments have Timestoppers, most of them reach their peak after five years or so. After that, they decline very quickly and are no good to any government agency for major missions, this is when they are at their greatest risk, hence the intrusion into their bodies at the very beginning. Their stories if ever allowed to come out, would astonish the world, and probably destabilise it.

I search for good potential, long term Timestoppers, who can continue to work for over ten years. if they wished, with not so taxing projects, but after that, they are not simply put to one side. No, no, they are on the payroll to help the next batch of transferred stoppers who feel violated by their agencies and have been given a bad time by their governments, there has to be a way out for all."

John nodded in agreement, to everything Victor had said, and he now knew his own course of action. He was frightened, yes, but was willing to trust someone, who he didn't really know, to remove something that could potentially kill him. Victor seemed like a caring a man, giving the impression he was there to help other people like John. The alternative was not so appealing, a government department, who had countless means at their disposal, and the sole use of more Timestoppers than John ever thought ever existed. It didn't warrant any kind consideration, simply, no contest, Victor wins.

Chapter 18

Wandsworth was uneasy, he pulled a seat up for Roper, "Yeah, I know he's been a bad boy, but he's one of the best operatives we've got for now." Roper replied.

"Do you know who he's with'?"

"Yes, I know."

"Look Roper, this department doesn't run around for John McAndrew. But Wordsworth, he knows far too much, unlike the others, he is more inquisitive, and he asks the right questions."

"The thing is, what do we do with him now, the stupid fucking Russian has got him, and god knows where, our sources say his phone has been tracked to a filling station in Croydon."

"For fucks sake, we are a major intelligence agency and we've fuckin lost him."

"He's gone"

"Well you better find him."

"He's really pissing me off now."

"We haven't got time for this fucking stupid game.
No doubt the Russian will be finding this most
amusing and stuffing Johns head full of stories
about, devices in his body etcetera, etcetera."

"What a load of shit! I just hope McAndrew has got
more sense than that. I know one thing, it's time to
inform the commander with this one, and I know he
fuckin hates that Russian, he's not gonna like it."

Wandsworth knocked on the door of the Senior
Operational Commander,

"Yes, Gordon, just a second." raising his head from
some top-secret papers, "What is it?" He told the
commander all about the disappearance of John
McAndrew.

"Do we know the Russian has him for definite?
bloody shit, that fucking Petrov, he's a fuckin pest.
Do we need a termination on McAndrew?" The
Commander looked inquisitively? "Gordon, just say,
your experienced enough, no one is that important."
A long silence prevailed while Wandsworth thought,

rubbing his chin, "No sir, we need him back here. Petrov cannot have him, he's too good, he just needs to be brought into line."

"Right then Gordon, I think this is reasonable, if he has been given all of Petrov's claptrap, hidden phials of nerve agent, and all that shite, McAndrew would have probably joined the little Russian gang by now, and he would be no fucking good to us. Tell you what, here's the deal, I'll give you forty-eight hours to get him back, or I'll have no option but to enforce a termination."

"Yes sir, that's fine, I totally agree." Wandsworth left quickly down the corridor, knowing he must somehow find John and convince him to return, Mr McAndrew's life was hanging in the balance.

Victor bid goodnight to John and headed for the lift, only John had other ideas and went for another drink, he certainly needed it. Glancing around there wasn't a lot of people around, so he settled himself at the bar. The bar tender offered conversation, but

John's mind was elsewhere. There was no going back now and something told him it wasn't going to be a happy ever after story, with that, he finished his drink and headed for his room.

The late shift at the hotel were busying away, turning down rooms and preparing for another day. Shortly after lying in his bed, tired but not asleep, a rustling at the door attracted his attention, he watched as a note was pushed under the door, thinking it was probably breakfast or the newspaper order. He couldn't sleep so he made himself a drink and retrieved the paper. It was a handwritten note with a phone number on it and signed by Catina, "Please contact me, urgent." What was this all about, she was reported dead by Grenville, there was only one way to find out.

The phone rang for what seemed like ages and then that familiar voice answered, "Hello John, how are you? I don't want to talk on the phone, can you meet me at..." and she reeled off an address which John hurriedly wrote down. He made his way to the address downtown, that he was given, which was an apartment block that was quite run down and dark.

It wasn't the place he was expecting at all. He rang the access panel and the door loudly buzzed open. Finding the flat, the door was answered by the still beautiful Catina.

"Mr McAndrew." she hugged John very tightly, as if she was his sister.

"Catina, what on earth has happened, I thought you were dead."

"John, I am still fighting the cause, and I am pleased to say, my false trail of my own death worked very well. We don't have much time so I will get straight to the point, Victor Petrov is a liar, he is a high ranking Russian agent who preys on people like yourself, with your skills. There is no drug inside you, what he says is to get you into a position where his own doctors can actually put a drug phyle into your body, and then blackmail you to work for the Russians. If you disagree with the regime, he will release the agent and kill you, there is no doubt about that. What he has said about your government is simply not true. I knew he had contacted you; I know he sounds genuine and I know you have been getting a hard time from your superiors, but please don't go through with any this. I have been watching your back now since our mission together, which you completed, and a cause that is dear to my heart, so I am indebted to you.

There are still many things you don't know regarding friends and foes, I cannot give any of this information, it's better for you, not to know. All I can do is protect you if I can, if you will allow me. Our world has more dark sides than good, and I will be your light through it all. My advice now is to make your way to the airport and get the first flight out of here, to go anywhere. Sort it out with your department and take the flack, and always be guarded. Victor won't give up, your commanders will know this and put things in place to help, but always be aware. If you need me, buy a phone and call this number. Now go and get away from all of this. Hopefully, we will speak soon." John gave Catina a huge hug and said goodbye.

He came out of the airport shop with a small case, not a thing in it, for all he had, was what he was standing in. "The only flight we have out tonight is to Belfast sir. I can get you on that, any baggage?" "No" John replied, feeling uneasy and out of place. "It will be boarding soon at gate sixteen sir, have a good evening."

John sat in the departure lounge, shaking, remembering all what Catina had said, it was beginning to sink in. Phone in hand, he knew he had to call the department. *"This is gonna be shite,"* the number rang and rang, *"Oh fuck, no!"* Grenville answered, *"He must be on a late duty,"* A tired yeah, came through the speaker. "It's McAndrew, Grenville I'm sorry about this..." he was trying to continue when Grenville stopped him, "Where are you and are you alone."

"Yeah, I'm alone and I'm in Geneva but I'm heading to Belfast." Waiting for the reaction, but nothing. Grenville was the calmest he had ever heard him, "We'll get you in Belfast." John gave him the flight number and the line went dead.

Chapter 19

Stepping off the military aircraft arriving from Belfast, he was ushered into a waiting land rover. Turning into the base he knew this was it, the bollocking of his life and he prepared himself for trouble from all sides.

Roper met him at the department doors. John looked around, ready for a surprise outburst from Grenville, but strangely he wasn't there. "You okay, John? everything fine? Consider this a de-brief rather than a reprimand, we need to know about the Russian what he said, what he did, what he suggested, had planned, implied, every fucking thing. We've got all the time in the world with this. I take it, you figured out his patter was shit, about the nerve agent etcetera."

John sheepishly nodded.

"What you must remember is, believe it or not, we

are looking out for you, we want you to be the best and to give your country the best. Leave the Russian to us, go home, chill out and remember who has your back. You'll have protection over the next few weeks or at least until Petrov gets the message, if we could find him and capture him, we would kill him, you know that, don't you?" John bowed his head; death didn't mean anything to these desensitised people.

Once he got home, he went straight to bed but with everything going on, he couldn't sleep and this was becoming more common. He got up out of bed and went to the bathroom, where he kept his trusted sleeping tablets, his ticket to a brilliant journey of peace and tranquillity.

The next morning, he awoke, realising he was in the safety of his own home, diving for a crack in the curtains, he confirmed a pair of plain clothes officers at the bottom of his drive, which reassured him. Suddenly, awareness came to the fore front, and the severity of what could have been, slammed into him like a ton of bricks, he immediately broke down into an emotional meltdown, tears falling down his cheeks. The fear and anxiety were overwhelming. His life was a mess, but what could he do? Whatever way he tried, it fell apart, he really believed Victor could have been the answer, he thought it could have been the sensible way out, shocked by the outcome, and surprised by Victor and the extents he was about to go to. John thought he was beginning to know him, but what happened over the past few weeks was all part of a massive learning curve which he needed to establish for himself, the outcome? Trust no one. With the exception of Catina, who he was certain would not lie or mislead him, he knew that there was a connection between them, they had an understanding, it was like a brother and sister relationship, but this still didn't stop him admiring her attractiveness.

His mobile buzzed, incoming message, he read it, from Victor: "I'm always here if you need me" John in a rage, smashed the phone across the table demolishing it into small pieces, bastard, he doesn't give up.

The weeks turned into months, slowly getting himself together, trying to forget what happened. The occasional visits from Lauren, made him feel a lot better. The weekly updates from the department came, but there were no missions, no targets, this suited him fine. He thought they must be giving him a well-earned rest, but why? he just didn't know. He was enjoying the peace, and the knowing he was safe. There had been no more communications from Victor, so John assumed he had perhaps moved on to another willing victim. John and the department were totally unaware for the past few weeks they had been under twenty-four hour surveillance by Victor Petrov's Russian team, and their net was tightening.

―――――――――――――――――

"I'm telling you; he must go." Said Victor

"I know him, I know how he thinks."

"He will never defect to us."

"He feels tricked."

"I don't want him."

"If we need to, we'll Timestop him, otherwise, he must be forced."

"But Roper's not having him either, so he must go."

"It's such a shame Dr Petrov, he was very good, one of the best ones I've seen in a while." The conversation went back and forth between Petrov and his top security advisor. "We've got others coming up, Pavel, and this is not worth the effort, put a plan in place and let me know, I will brief our commanders."

John was busy making breakfast when his doorbell chimed into action, being cautious he checked from the window, *"My god, I am privileged."* Both Gordon Wandsworth and Roper stood on his doorstep, *"What the hell do they want?"* John opened the door.

"What an honour this is."

"Alright McAndrew, don't get clever, we're here to see how you are. Are you feeling back to your old self now?"

"And, what old self is that Mr Wandsworth? you mean, before I got enlisted by you lot? Or a normal person?"

Wandsworth stared John out, "Listen your ungrateful bastard, remember who you're talking to, where here for your protection and well-being."

Roper quietly said, "We have been looking at your latest medical reports and realise how hard you are finding this mentally. We know how difficult it can be when you're not military trained so after consideration we have a contract for you, which I guarantee will be your last, you can refuse, and carry on with your work, but if you do this one job, we will cut you loose, release all ties and rehome you wherever you want in the world, no more missions."

John started laughing, "Are you kidding?" John laughed, "I just been conned by a top Russian agent and you're making it out as if everything is alright. Who am I to trust? Let's guess, I know, I'm gonna trust no one and that includes you?"

"This is a genuine offer John, have a think on it, small job near your old home turf, a simple job then your redundant. Have a think overnight and I'll call you in the morning. Oh, here's a new mobile, and before you ask, yes, its monitored." With that, the two of them left John's house and departed down the lane, but Russian eyes were not far behind them, armed with a full dialog from Johns house.

Driving back to the office, conversation was in full flow about John. "He's wised up now Gordon, I don't think he'll buy our relocation story, it's been too close to Petrov's little caper." We need to be careful; we must get him to accept the terms, then get him in the right place for the hit." Responded Gordon

"This could go tits up if it's not done right."

"I totally agree, we need to make this look like it's come from the Russians."

"Obviously. Victor would be prime suspect."

"McAndrews's got no allies now, and he's got no idea his girlfriend Lauren is one of our undercovers."

"You know something Roper? That might work in our favour, if we can get her involved, she could use a bit of influence that might just swing it, we'll have a meeting with her tomorrow." "Has she any genuine ties to him?"

"Are you kidding, she's married anyway. Her hubby's in the States in special forces. She is ruthless, she would sell her mother, no, no we won't have any problem there."

It was lashing down with rain outside, a dreadful dismal day and John came in like a drowned rat. The phone was ringing continually, "Alright, alright, I'm bloody coming." He picked the phone up full of hell, but quickly calmed when he realised it was Lauren.

"Hi John, how are you today?" Lots of small talk

followed and Lauren suggested she would come over tonight, for some supper and stayover. John knew what that meant and quickly agreed. He hastily prepared the place, candles, wine chilling, and all in all looking quite romantic. When she arrived, Lauren looked a little bit anxious, John asked what was wrong? was everything okay?

"I need to tell you something John." *oh god! he thought, it's dumping time.* "I'll get straight to the point; I have been asked to head up a finance operation in New Zealand and have been given very little time to consider my options. The package on the table is out of this world. House, excellent salary, but if I choose yes, I will be going in less than a month. This is a chance of a lifetime, but I want it for us, not just me, we have been so good together and I love you so much. I don't want to start all over again, thousands of miles apart, you wouldn't be able to come over there every weekend."

John's arms shot around her, and gave a reassuring

hug, "Don't worry, I'm not letting you go anywhere without me. I'm sure I will be able to sort something out. Maybe, if I have a word with your boss, with me being freelance, he may sign me up to go with you." Lauren stopped the tears, thinking seed planted.

"Come on my darling, everything will be fine." hugging and kissing, "Look, I'm going with you, even if I must throw the towel in here. I'll get fixed up over there." laughing he said, "Maybe I'll even work for you? The moods changed to giggling and there romantic evening continued.

John checked into the department and headed for Wandsworth's door. "Hi John, I was just about to call you. Well then, have you slept on our discussion and offer?"
"I have, Mr Wandsworth, but I have a few conditions, if they are agreed I am prepared to be relocated, I would like to go to New Zealand as soon as possible. My conditions are mainly financial, but, one stipulation, you need to assure me, there will be

no future contact, I don't want it. I don't want to be considered a Timestopper anymore, I want a normal, well near as normal life as I can have. Any missions, contracts or even end of the world scenarios, I just don't want to know, is that any good?"

"John, myself and this department will have no problem with any of your needs. Personally, I hope you have a good life in New Zealand and you settle well, but one thing you must remember, you have signed the official secrets act and you will be tongue tied for the rest of your life. Failure to keep within these boundaries, the smallest story, a snippet of information leaked to the press, anything you have seen or done for this department, will make you a covert target of this government, and you above all, should know what that implies, is that okay?"

"That's fine." said John.

"Right, if you go to the briefing room, and see Grenville, he'll tell you about your last mission with us, and John, good luck, and it really has been nice knowing you."

Chapter 20

"Mr McAndrew." announced Grenville. "Come on in and make yourself comfortable. Now, I'm led to believe this is your last outing with this unit…"

John interrupted, "Or any other bloody unit."

"Okay son, don't get shirty. Let's see if we can be civil and get down to business."

"Sorry, can we just get on with it, please?"

"Right." he threw the file across to John, "Do you know this?"

"Sure." came the reply. John studied the map of the underground, on it there were two stations circled. Clacton hill and the next stop Stamford Court.

"Yeah, okay". Grenville started the brief.

"Background first. It seems we have a terrorist freedom fighter on our hands. This gentleman has obtained, by whatever means, some Sarin chemical compound. You may recall a similar substance used in 1995 in Japan. Well, we have very strong intel that our target has produced this stuff and is about to make his mark in the terrorist world by releasing this into our tube network, which obviously would kill hundreds if not thousands of people in the aid of his cause. Now we can't just arrest this man as we are told he carries the substance in a glass bottle wherever he goes for fear of attack. We will have a very short time window with this, and all I can say is, it will be next week when the City Carnival is on, releasing it then, will make maximum impact."

John spent a little time going over the folder as Grenville continued to talk, "He is under twenty-four hour observation and we may have to jump on this at short notice. Your part in this is simple really, get on the train, stop time and retrieve the bottle from the suspect, and place it in an evidence bag. Get off the train, and pass the bag to waiting security staff, there, job done, okay?"

"It's always seems so easy with you Grenville. It could slip from my hands, or it could just smash."

"Well if it did, it would be, bye, bye, Mr McAndrew. Here's the rest of the details and contacts. I'll see you next week and enjoy your final mission dumb shit. By the way, you'll receive details of your redundancy soon."

"Thanks for all the time and effort you've offered me over the years Grenville". Grenville just glanced and stuck his fingers up.

John spoke to Lauren, "We're all set to go, I'm all sorted at work, and I'm coming with you darling." Lauren was overjoyed at the news. Knowing Roper and Wandsworth had done their part, now she, in her usual ruthless way was spurting happiness at John like a cobra waiting to give the final strike.

"When can we go?" She asked.

"It looks like I've just got a few things to sort out, so probably next month."

"Brilliant." She said, "It's all working out now John, I can feel our lives getting back together the way it should be. I'll see you tomorrow night, love you."

"Love you back." Then the line went dead.

Lauren immediately texted a USA number. "Hey sweetie it looks like I'll be with you next month. Got this case on its final run and nearly closed. I'll be home soon."

It was the day of the City Carnival in town, and John's phone buzzed, it was Grenville, "It's definitely today, so get yourself down to the Stamford Court tube station, that's where you will be required. Wear the earpiece that was given to you, your military contacts know who you are. Keep the radio on and concealed in your pocket, your call sign is Fox One. The instructions will be straight forward."

"Okay, on my way." Breakfast aborted, John hooked up the security radio and earpiece and set off for Stamford Court tube station.

On arrival at the tube station, it was very busy, John's radio was hissing, and occasional voices would be heard, "Fox One if you can hear us nod your head." John obliged.

"Okay, make your way to the platform, when instructed you'll need the first carriage, we have eyes on the train and on you." Again, John nodded. Standing on the platform, he could feel a waft of air, signalling the arrival of a train. "It's not this one." a voice said in the earpiece. The train charged in and commuters got on and off in the busy morning rush hour.

"Fox One, I can confirm it is the next train, I repeat, the next train, first carriage, white male, backpack with orange tee shirt, facing the doors." The familiar waft of air came, and the train roared into and stopped on the platform. "Fox One, when those doors open do your thing."

John followed the instruction stopping time as the

doors were fully open. He walked into the carriage and saw the target. He carefully manoeuvred himself in front of the guy and patting his pockets he realised something was in the right hand coat pocket. He slipped his hand inside and pulled out a small bottle of liquid. Carefully he carried the bottle from the train and placed it into an evidence bag he had in his hand ready. He started time, and all hell broke loose, loads of security officers boarded the train and removed the target. A very tall burly officer came to John hand open, "The Bottle." John gave him the evidence bag. All over in minutes, the train was on its way again, he looked around, everyone gone.

He was about to phone Lauren when all of a sudden, he came over sweaty, a bit like it was in the early stopping days. He didn't feel well at all, feeling tired, He needed fresh air he thought, and headed across the street to the park. Grabbing some water from his bag, he sat down on one of the benches, feeling so dizzy, nauseous, *"What the hell is happening to me?"* A member of the public spoke to him, "Are you okay mate?" John wanted to speak but couldn't get the words out. He felt himself slipping to the ground, in and out of consciousness, he could hear paramedics talking to him, and then sharp jolts across his body. He was swiftly loaded into the waiting ambulance.

Grenville put the phone down and addressed Wandsworth, "As expected sir, everything went according to plan. A good exercise for the squad as well. McAndrew didn't have a clue the bottle was full of water but coated in nerve agent, it would have soaked into his skin super quick. He would have stood no chance; the stupid bastard even gave us the bottle back. If it does what it says, Mr McAndrew will no longer be with us, poor sod."

"It's very good stuff." said Wandsworth, "Totally untraceable, excellent. He was a good Timestopper though, in fact, very good. He was just getting to be too much of a risk, and we can't have that can we? Plenty more where he came from."

Roper nodded; "I've got some good ones coming

up."

The doors flung open and Paramedics rushed through the corridor to a rather full Accident and Emergency department at Ashford General. "Cardiac Arrest." Shouted one of the paramedics. The crash team moved swiftly into action, like ants around their new arrival. "Listen up!" the authority of a senior doctor called out, "We've got John McAndrew; arrested twenty minutes ago, re-sussed by medics and has relapsed again." A string of medical jargon followed; each piece digested by the carefully placed professionals. Machines buzzed and beeped into action, to save this young man's life, which sadly, was slowly slipping away from him.

Senior A&E Doctor, Dr James Wilde was now calling the shots, machine gun like instructions were being followed to the letter by his staff. As the valuable seconds turned into long minutes which slowly ebbed away, there was no respite in the anxiety for their patient. As if time had given those around him a limited slot, the ping of the heart monitor was no longer echoing round the room, it had suddenly changed to a straight deathly tone, just an alarm light flashing. They all looked around at each other, no response from the team, and no response from their patient. Despite all the efforts, it looked like Mr McAndrews, was to be another sad statistic of death by cardiac arrest.

Dr Wilde let out those inevitable words, "Let's call it, no pulse, no brain activity. It's been too long now. Time of death, 12:45 p.m. Right team, thanks for your efforts but let's move along quickly, the world doesn't stop here."

"Hello Dr Petrov, Sir, I can confirm the target is dead." said one of the paramedics standing outside the hospital entrance. "No Sir we didn't get time to achieve our goal, but it would seem it has been done for us. Okay, thank you, sir." The paramedic hung up as did Victor

Back in the resus area, the team were moving on to another patient, and an assistant was scurrying around John's lifeless body. She looked around to make sure that she was alone, then pulling out a syringe from her pocket she quickly supplied his vein, with lots of hope, and life-saving drugs.

It was hastily removed, and she pressed the emergency button on the wall. Soon the room was filled once again, she told the doctor, that John had spoken to her. Immediately procedures were put into action. The ward exit doors swung back and forth, as a young pretty girl from Romania quietly left the hospital. Leaving behind confused emergency staff and a patient who's heart was racing to catch up with time.

Mr John Macandrew was about to begin a new life.

Printed in Poland
by Amazon Fulfillment
Poland Sp. z o.o., Wrocław

52657831R00137